○○○

"WE HIT THE ROAD, FIRST," CONTI SAID.

"Then cross five hundred yards of open field. We'll cross, at the railroad, two at a time. One man covers while the other makes his play."

Price said, "For a man who's absobloodylutely crackers, you're certainly getting cautious, mate. You're marching us right to a Nazi prison camp, and you worry about crossing a flaming railway! You really must be off your chump!"

"The planes will be there to pick us up," said Conti, stubbornly.

Price shook his head and said, "Right. There are fairies in the bottom of my garden, too! Can't you see the lot of us are expendable, mate? We've done the perishing job they sent us to do. There's no reason for them to worry about us, now. We're only little chaps, you see. Nobody gives a damn what happens to the likes of us!"

○○○

can repair a lot of radiator leaks before you know what's wrong, and sooner or later, the engine has to be scrapped.

Fawcett Gold Medal Books
by Lou Cameron:

SKY RIDERS

DROP INTO HELL

DROP INTO HELL

Lou Cameron

A FAWCETT GOLD MEDAL BOOK

Fawcett Publications, Inc., Greenwich, Connecticut

DROP INTO HELL

ISBN 0-449-13611-6

Printed in the United States of America

10   9   8   7   6   5   4   3   2   1

DROP
INTO
HELL

10 9 8 7 6 5 4 3 2 1

○○○

NORFOLK, ENGLAND, 1944 . . . It was April Fool's Day
and the Tall General was drunk. Not drunk enough to
keep him from doing the job he had to do. Just drunk
enough to dull the edge of his conscience. His WAC secretary came into the small briefing room to say, "Captain
Evans is waiting, darling," and the Tall General said, "Let
him wait. And don't call me darling while you're on duty,
damn it!"

The WAC smiled and snapped to mocking attention,
thrusting her chest out as far as she could. She was well
aware that her chest was one of her better features. Her
face was all right. But it was her figure and ability to keep
her mouth shut that had made her the Tall General's girl
Friday.

The general tried to frown at her. But instead he
laughed and said, "Cut it out. You're giving me a hard-on.
You know what's getting to me about this mess, don't
you?"

"Your hard-on, darling? I know how to take care of that!"

"Damn it, kitten, I told you to stop fooling around. I've got that poor asshole waiting out there to get his head blown off, and I dunno, it's starting to get to me. I have to *con* the poor slob, kitten. I have to con Evans and his men into thinking they have a better chance than a snow-ball in hell!"

The woman shrugged and said, "It's been a shitty war. But at least it's almost over, dear."

"Hitler's got at least a year's mileage left on him," said the Tall General, picking up a manila 201 file and scan-ning through it. "David Evans, Captain AUS, ROTC Colorado School of Mines . . . It's that Colorado School of Mines that bought him this ticket, you know. The poor slob should have studied dentistry. We'd have never picked a dentist for this mission . . ."

The WAC said, "You're stalling, darling. It's not going to do him any good to wait outside all day."

The Tall General sighed and said, "Show him in." Then, as the woman left, he went to a filing cabinet, took out a bottle of black market Canadian, and had a stiff belt from the bottle.

He'd just closed the filing cabinet again and turned around when the WAC came back in with a slender young man in paratrooper kit. Captain Evans brought the heels of his jump boots together with a dull click and managed half a salute before the Tall General cut him off with, "As you were, Dave. We haven't time for that West Point bullshit. Do you know what you're doing here?"

Dave Evans smiled and answered, "Something about a secret mission, sir?"

The Tall General said, "More like a secret fucking mess." He turned to an acetate-covered map on the wall and added, "Come over here and see what the purple-pissing Nazis have been up to now."

Evans joined the older man in front of the map as the WAC watched from across the room. The paratrooper was cute, she thought, and he looked like he'd be a tiger in bed too. It seemed such a shame that the war used up all the cute ones and left the fat and bald old farts alive. She wondered if the captain had a girl, and if there was any chance she could get him alone before he jumped. How long did they have anyway, and would the Tall General have him under security surveillance until he took off?

The map on the wall was a large-scale contour chart of Central Europe. The acetate overlay was covered with red marks, made by a grease pencil. The Tall General swept a finger down a line of red circles and explained, "These big Os stand for oil. The smaller letters give the type of installation. With D-Day set for sometime this summer, we're going after Hitler's fuel supplies. G2 tells us they have at least two new tanks that can kick the shit out of our Mark Fives, and they're working on a fighter that can do 600 miles and hour. Our P-51 does, what, 400 tops?"

Evans nodded and said, "Guy from the Eighth Air Force was telling me Jerry has a new rocket ship of some kind. Sounds sort of Buck Rogers, if you ask me."

The Tall General swore and said, "I'm not asking you. I'm telling you what G2 says we have to worry about, and even if they don't have their jet fighters in production yet, those ME-109s and FW-190s are still rolling off the assembly line."

Evans nodded and said, "But they can't go anywhere if they don't have any fuel. I get the picture, sir."

The general grimaced and said, "Right. Fuel for his tinker toys is Hitler's weak spot. We've got enough petroleum to drown the cocksucker in, and he's got the Danube oil fields, period. The Russians took the Baku fields back from Adolf, and we've been bombing the shit out of his oil wells at Ploesti. But there's a nigger in the woodpile. The fucking Krauts have been making gas and oil out of *coal*. Did they teach you anything about coal hydrogenation at that mining school in Colorado, captain?"

Evans nodded and said, "Yessir, it's called the Haber process. Fritz Haber invented it back in 1913, along with a way of making ammonium nitrate from thin air and electricity. The Haber ammonia process was swiped for the British in time for World War I. We're still using it to make explosives for this war. But Haber's coal hydrogenation ideas never amounted to much. It costs about fifty cents a gallon to make gasoline that way, and with the stuff costing eleven cents FOB Texas . . ."

"Hitler doesn't have an oil field in Texas," the Tall General cut in. "The whole fucking Luftwaffe's running on *coal*. The British tell us the Nazis have about a dozen of these hydrogenation plants cranking out high-octane fuel for their air force. We've been bombing the shit out of them all winter, and G2 says they're starting to hurt. Production is down to where a lot of Krauts are having to walk. If we can cut it down some more by D-Day, they'll *all* have to walk. You see our problem?"

Evans nodded and scanned the map as he asked, "Why can't we just keep bombing them until they're all out of business, sir?"

"Because we don't know where all of them are, and because they got very cute with this one motherfucker here!"

The Tall General stabbed a finger at a spot on the map and continued, "This installation is called Fabrik Vogelbach. It's as far up the Rhine as you can get a coal barge without running into Swiss territory. The Swiss have been acting very standoffish since we bombed Zurich by mistake that time. So the position of the plant is a little nervous making, even if they hadn't put the fucking plant between two other targets we just can't drop a bomb on. Come over here and I'll show you a blowup."

Evans followed the Tall General to a map table and

stared down at a photo-montage mounted on bristol board. A medium-sized factory complex occupied about two-thirds of a small valley running into the Rhine. Tucked between the factory complex and the valley wall was a cluster of buildings with white roofs. The photos were in black and white. But the Red Cross emblem was unmistakable at this scale. The Tall General said, "Yeah, it's a German field hospital. The cute part is that they have some wounded British and American flyers there. It's a showpiece, supervised by the International Red Cross. Couple of Swiss nationals in residence. So I don't have to tell you what a diplomatic flap we get into if so much as a window gets broken on that side of the target."

Evans nodded and pointed to what seemed to be a more military installation on the other side of the factory complex. He asked, "What's this, sir, a German army camp?"

"No. That's the Vogelbach Concentration Camp. It's full of Jews and Gypsies rounded up in Eastern Europe in the last four years. It's another showpiece, like the hospital. We've gotten reports about other camps that just have to be British propaganda. But the Gestapo's been putting on a smile for those same Red Cross jerks from over the border. The Vogelbach CC specializes in women and children. They've rounded up a lot of adorable tykes and healthy young prisoners who can put away three square meals a day. They have the adults working in the coal hydrogenation plant or tending the kids. Every time the Red Cross gets a report on Dachau or Buchenwald, the purple-pissing Nazis invite them over to Vogelbach for a full inspection. The British have it that the prisoners are being coddled, by German standards. One of the SS guards raped a Jewish girl last summer and was publicly executed for doing it. You just can't beat a Kraut for being two-faced."

Evans frowned and said, "In other words, if we bomb

that coal hydrogenation plant, we're bound to kill innocent prisoners and cause an international incident!"

"Screw the innocent prisoners. It's the international incident we have to worry about!"

Then he asked, "How would you drop in there and take that fuel plant out of action without, repeat, *without* making a lot of noise?"

"That's what you want me to do, sir? I mean, France is still occupied! We'd be jumping right smack in the middle of Hitler's Europe!"

"So?"

"So how in blue blazes do we get back to our own lines, sir?"

The Tall General didn't look at Evans as he said, "We'll get to that in a minute, captain. By the way, it's going to be *major,* with a DSM, if you pull this off. The question is can you do it? Can you put that fucking plant out of business without blowing the whole valley sky high?"

Evans frowned and said, "I have to think. I know the process in theory. You start with a bed of pulverized coal, heated to at least 2000 degrees. You inject live steam into the incandescent carbon. The next stage is synthesis gas, a white-hot mixture of hydrogen and carbon monoxide. If we were to sabotage that end of the plant, it would take off for the nearest planet!"

Evans thought a moment before he continued, "Let's see. . . . The synthesis gas jets into a catalytic chamber, where it cools off and turns to liquid hydrocarbon. It's a black gunk that looks and acts like crude petroleum. You pump that into a regular cracking tower and separate it by fractional distillation. You wind up with alcohol, gasoline, diesel fuel, lubricating oil, wax, and so forth, down to asphalt."

"What happens if you sabotage the cracking towers?"

"While they're full of boiling hydrocarbon, sir? They'd take off like rockets, if we were lucky and they didn't go off like king-sized bombs. Pound for pound, *petroleum* packs more power than dynamite, if it goes off all at once!"

"So, we'd be just as well off if we bombed the fucking plant?"

Dave Evans was tempted. But he shook his head and said, "I think the weak link in the chain would be the catalytic chambers, sir. Destroy them and you get a reasonably small explosion right in the center of the plant. There'd be one hell of a fire. The hot gas shooting out of the coal retorts would have the thermal energy of regular cooking gas back home. You'd have a super blowtorch shooting out a few hundred feet or so, until they could get the fire under control. I wouldn't want to be anywhere in the middle of the installation when that happened. But I don't think the damage would extend much beyond the plant itself."

The Tall General smiled and said, "I knew I could count on you, son. You have a platoon of paratroopers to get you into the joint. What do you need to thigamajig that, ah, catalyst thing?"

Evans said, "I need an *expert*, sir. I need a man who's been *inside* a place like Fabrik Vogelbach."

"I thought you said you know how the damned plant works!"

"I do, sir. But only on paper! Have you ever been inside an oil refinery complex, sir? It's a regular jungle of pipes and valves, even to a stranger who's been working in another plant. I have no idea what to look for. I could probably tell a catalyst chamber from a retort, given time to study the layout. But I don't know what sort of catalyst the Germans use. I don't know which pipes go where or what valve opens what. I could maybe plant some charges and hope for the best. But you're asking me to take apart a watch with a sledge hammer. I have no idea what might happen if we just sail in there and start ripping things apart!"

The general raised a hand to silence Evans and said, "I'll ask upstairs for somebody that knows his catalyst from a hole in the ground. Meanwhile, I've been going over the list of volunteers you sent me. They've all been checked out by CIC. But I have a couple of names I want you to scratch. I don't want you to take Corporal Zukerman or Sergeant Marvin on this mission, son."

Evans frowned and said, "I understand about Zukerman, sir. You don't ask a Jew to jump into the middle of Germany. But what's your objection to Roy Marvin? He's got a hell of a record and he speaks a little German. I was sort of counting on Marvin as my platoon sergeant!"

"I know the guy from North Africa and Sicily," said the Tall General. "I decorated the kid after Wadi Gemal, and in those days, he was a hell of a soldier."

"In those days, sir?"

"Marvin's made three combat jumps. Two in Africa and one in Sicily last year. He won that Silver Star for taking over after his unit was nearly wiped out in North Africa. When the troops jumped into Sicily, Marvin's outfit bought a 94 percent casualty rate, and they say he doesn't salute officers anymore unless they're wearing paratrooper boots."

Evans smiled and said, "I'm wearing paratrooper boots, sir. Marvin's a little snotty. But he's one hell of a fighting machine."

"Not anymore. Not after three combat jumps. One or two are all any of you are good for, son. Some men may have three jumps in them before they get used up. Nobody has four. I want you to replace Marvin and Zukerman. Any other questions?"

Evans nodded and said, "Yessir. You still haven't told me how I get my people *out* of there, once we complete the mission!"

"You'll be told before you take off," said the Tall General, and again his eyes refused to meet those of the younger man.

He handed Evans an envelope and said, "You'd better get in touch with the British flyers you'll be working with. This is to be a joint Anglo-American mission, as I told you before. The RAF's been jury-rigging three British bombers as transports, but they have funny ideas about jumping out of planes. You'll want to familiarize yourselves with their procedure. I don't want you to tell your men too much about the mission before you're ready to take off. But you may want a few dry runs with the planes you'll be jumping from and . . ."

"Sir!" Evans cut in, "I have to give them some idea of what they volunteered for. Most of them thought, as I did, we were dropping just across the channel ahead of D-Day. I'm not sure all of them would be willing, if they knew just how deep into Germany I'm taking them!"

The Tall General reddened and snapped, "It's a little late in this war for us to be getting choosy about our missions, captain! You and your men volunteered for this particular mission when you volunteered for the fucking paratroops! Do you think we issued you those silver wings and snazzy boots just so you could get laid more often than the other boys?"

"Nossir, but . . ."

"But me no buts, captain! You guys have been strutting around lording it over us lesser mortals while you draw twice the pay of regular infantrymen! You think you're the cream of this man's army, and maybe, just maybe, you're right! But we didn't train you and jazz you up just so's we'd have prettier soldiers than anybody else on our side, captain! We sent you to Benning to make *paratroopers* out of you. Paratroopers are not made to beat up quartermasters and screw all the women in the ETO. Paratroopers are made for paratroop missions, and there was nothing in the contract about anyone getting to *choose* said missions. Do you read me, mister?"

A muscle twitched in the younger man's jaw. But his voice was calm as he replied, "Yessir. Will that be all, sir?"

"Yeah. All for now at any rate. Get in contact with your air crews, and I'll see about that petroleum expert you say you need. Meanwhile, you figure to jump within seventy-two hours, whether I can get him or not!"

The WAC secretary waited until Evans had left, dark with suppressed anger, before she turned to the Tall General and said, "I remember Sergeant Marvin, dear. He's that big good-looking moose with the scar from North Africa. Why didn't you want him to go along with Captain Evans and the others? Did CIC raise a fuss about him having German ancestry or something?"

The general shrugged and went to the filing cabinet, saying, "Marvin's only part German. He'll probably win another medal on D-Day. Christ, I'm dying for another drink!"

As he opened the cabinet and got out the bottle, the woman insisted, "That's not what you just told Captain Evans, dear. You said the sergeant was all used up."

"For this kind of a mission, he is," said the general, uncorking the bottle and taking a stiff belt. He came up for air to add owlishly, "Sergeant Marvin and that other kid, Zukerman, are *survivors*. They both came out of that mess in Sicily alive, and when the casualty rate's running 94 percent, that takes more than guts. That takes *brains!*"

"So? What's the matter with a soldier having brains, hon?"

The Tall General grimaced and said, "A soldier with a brain is a contradiction in terms, my dear. You don't send old hands like Marvin and Zukerman on suicide missions. Old soldiers never die, because old soldiers know when you're trying to get them killed!"

The woman gasped and asked, "Are you really trying

to get that cute Captain Evans killed?"

The Tall General suddenly seemed a little older as he shrugged and answered, "I'm not trying to get anyone killed. This fucking war is doing it for me. I told Ike I'd put that Kraut refinery out of business well before D-Day, and D-Day will be any fucking minute now!"

"But why do they have to die?" the woman insisted. "You told him you had a way for him to get his men out, once they complete their mission."

"I lied," shrugged the Tall General. He took another gulp of Canadian and mused, "I lie a lot, you know. It's part of my job and I'm very good at it. I guess that's why they made me a general in the first place."

forbidding you to do it. But the orders won't get here before you take off."

○○○

The rusty old tramp steamer would have been cut up for scrap in normal times. But ships were worth their weight in gold on the North Atlantic run these days, and so she steamed into Liverpool, listing to starboard in the oily Mersey roads, with a deck cargo of crated fighter planes and a hold full of something very secret.

The skipper called Matt Price to the bridge as an unmarked launch drew alongside the still moving ship. Price came up out of the humid hell of the engine room, squinting in the light of day like some subterranean animal. The sky was dove gray over Liverpool, dotted with tethered barrage balloons that were supposed to keep the Jerry bombers high above the vital harbor mouth. Matt Price had his own opinions about his country's air defenses. But he'd learned, over the years, to keep such opinions to himself.

The skipper greeted him with a frown and asked, "What have you been up to, lad? There's a police launch coming alongside to fetch you! Did you do something over in yon States?"

Price shook his head and said, "I never left the ship in Hoboken, skipper. We were only tied up a few days, remember?"

The ship's master shrugged and said, "Well, we'll know in half a mo'. The bulls are coming over the side."

The two men climbing over the bulwark wore trench coats and no hats. When the bos'n conducted them to the bridge, Price noticed they wore dark olive uniforms under the trench coats. There was a gilt US on one of the visitor's collar tabs. The other wore no insignia of any kind. He flashed his wallet open at the skipper and snapped, "Leyland, here. From the Home Office." This other chap is Agent Brooks, American counterintelligence."

Leyland frowned at Owens and asked, "Would this be Mister Price?"

The skipper nodded and said, "Yes. What's he done that you lads should be after him for?"

"We'll explain in the launch," said Leyland. "Let's go, Mister Price. You have a train to catch."

"I have to get my things. Am I under arrest?"

"No to both questions, Mister Price. We'll send for your belongings when the ship docks. You're not in any trouble. You just volunteered to do a certain job in His Majesty's service. But, let's get cracking, shall we?"

Price blurted, "I volunteered *what?*" but didn't argue as the two of them half steered, half carried him to the boarding ladder. A crew member helped him over the side, muttering, "Coo, you've done it now, Price!" and the confused seaman tried to gather his thoughts as he clambered down to the swaying launch below.

He noticed the crew of the smaller craft were wearing Royal Navy kit, although the launch itself was nondescript. A crew member helped him to a seat in the open cockpit while another cast off. The mysterious pair who'd come to fetch him took up positions on either side and the American, Brooks, said, "I understand you're a member of the Communist Party, Price."

Matt Price shook his head and said, "I used to be, back in the thirties. Lots of lads in the Trade Union Movement were Marxists in those days, but . . ."

"You fought on the Communist side in the Spanish Civil War," insisted the American.

Price shrugged and said, "We called ourselves the International Brigade. Some of us might have been Reds. Other lads were just out to stop the bloody Fascists."

"You were a Communist," insisted Brooks flatly.

Leyland, from the Home Office, shook his head and said, "That was a long time ago, old boy, and Stalin is on our side these days. I'm sure Mister Price's political views are of no great importance right now."

"They will be," said the American. "As soon as this mess is over, we're gonna have to fight the fucking Commies! I trust that bastard Stalin about as far as I'd trust Hitler's brother. I don't see any difference between a Red and a Nazi anyway!"

Leyland smiled and said, "There's a great difference, old boy. The Nazis drop bombs on us. The Reds don't. It's all quite simple when you think about it."

The American swore under his breath and, turning to Price, said, "They tell us you're a whirling chemical genius of some kind. So how come you're only an oiler on that rusty tub back there, these days?"

Matt Price shrugged and answered, "You just answered your own question, Yank. His Majesty doesn't hand out commissions to known party members. A berth in the merchant marine was as much as I could ask, considering my record."

Leyland said, "We understand you left the Communist party in '39. Any particular reason?"

"I grew up," said Price. "That Soviet-Nazi pact to

divide up Poland sort of stuck in my craw, along with Stalin's invasion of Finland and so forth. But what's the use of my explaining? You lot have me down as a Red and that's that. I haven't asked anyone to forgive me for what I did in the days I thought this world was run on the level!"

Leyland nodded and said, "Right. What's done is done, eh? What do you know about coal hydrogenation, Mister Price? We understand you worked in such a plant one time."

"Spain in thirty-eight." Price nodded, explaining, "When the Internationals were cut off in the Sierra, I had to blend into the countryside to save my neck. I'd studied chemistry in school, and being from the Black Country in the first place, I knew a bit about coal. Got a job in a plant near Toledo. The Fascists later dismantled it and sent it to Italy to pay for the help they'd gotten from the Black Shirts. But they never suspected who I was. So they only fired me. Most of the lads I served with were shot. The Internationals were sold out, you know. The ruddy Reds used us as a rear guard and let us die to save their arses. You might say that was the beginning of my political reformation."

Leyland nodded impatiently and asked, "If you were to find yourself inside a coal hydrogenation plant somehow, do you imagine you'd know how to sabotage it?"

"Sure. Turn a few wrong valves and run like hell before the cracking towers blew."

"What about the catalytic chambers? You suppose you'd know how to destroy that part of the process?"

Price nodded and said, "Of course. But those chambers are simple to rebuild."

"How long would it take, assuming you did a real job on the catalytic part?"

Price frowned and said, "Six or eight weeks maybe. The hard part would be replacing the catalytic screening. The place I was at in Spain used a platinum-coated chrome steel. Perishing expensive stuff to replace, you know."

Leyland nodded and said, "The point is, you do know how to take the bloody things apart. You're just the man we need, Mister Price!"

Price looked around at the harbor as the launch moved up the Mersey and asked, "Where's this place I'm supposed to sabotage?"

The American, Brooks, said "Germany" before Leyland could stop him.

Price laughed and said, "You can drop me off at any landing, mates. I'm not about to volunteer for any such thing as a trip to Jerry-land!"

"You just did," said Leyland, smiling. "I daresay you'll find a full pardon reward enough for serving King and Country. But there's a Royal Commission and a bonus in it for you as well."

Price blinked in surprise and blurted, "A full pardon? . . . For what? For being a flaming fool when I was young?"

Leyland smiled, but his eyes were hard as he said, "For *murder*, Mister Price. Something about a chap who went overboard on your last voyage. They say you had words with that lascar lad, just before he vanished over the side one night!"

Price gasped, "Garn! I never! I don't know who in God's name took care of that thieving lascar sod! There were a dozen lads in that crew had better reasons than me for killing the ruddy Oriental!"

"Ah, but you were the only member of the crew with a criminal record, Mister Price. You have a record of violence and industrial sabotage in your past. Why, come to think of it, you're a ruddy *Communist!* How do you think that would go down with a jury, assuming you were fool enough to want to stand trial?"

For a long time Price said nothing as the launch puttered through the oily water toward the docks. Then he shrugged and said, "I guess I just volunteered, after all."

Leyland smiled and answered, "We thought you'd see your duty to King and Country, once it was explained to you properly."

ooo

The two British guards at the airdrome gate were startled to see a convoy of American trucks bearing down on them in the East Anglian twilight. One of the guards came unstuck in time to step out on the gravel road and shout "Hoy!" and the lead truck braked to a stop. The convoy behind folded like an accordion as each driver managed to stop his vehicle, and from under the canvas covers of the trucks, a chorus of cursing groans could be heard in the gathering gloom.

A Négro driver stuck his head out of the lead truck and the British guard said, "You made a wrong turn, mate. This is a bloody RAF base! Your lot belongs another mile or more down this road."

The Negro waved a clipboard and answered, "No they don't. I got me a mess of paratroopers to deliver to this here base. I got the trip ticket and I'm in a hurry. Don't want to drive these motherfucking six-by-sixes back in no blackout, can I help it!"

The guard came over and investigated the travel orders,

as somewhere in the convoy, someone urinated over a tailgate. The guard saw the Yanks had the right address, and it was no business of his why a platoon from the US Eighty-second Airborne had been ordered to a British airdrome. So he waved them through, shouting, "Up the road and turn left at the flagstaff, mate!"

The trucks drove slowly across the British bomber base as the lead driver searched for clues. The installation had been carved out of flat farmland, and the buildings had been camouflaged to look like farm buildings. The tarmac roads were laid out in an irregular sprawl, in hopes that Jerry might not spot the regular patterns of a military installation from the air.

Since there is no way to disguise a runway pattern, and since bomber hangars are much too large to pass for barns, the effort had been wasted on Jerry. It just made it hard to find your way about the base.

But someone had nailed a sign, reading Able Baker Unit, to a tree in front of a Nissen hut. So the convoy stopped. A flight sergeant in RAF blue came out of the hut and yelled, "Are you lot the lads from the Eighty-second?"

Pete Conti jumped down from the tailgate of the lead truck. He walked over to the flight sergeant and said, "I'm Pete Conti, platoon sergeant. Where do you want these guys?"

"I'm Wilkins," said the flight sergeant, waving at the hut in back of him as he added, "This will be your quarters while you lot are here. I'm to see that you're made comfortable. Have you lot eaten yet?"

Conti smiled and replied, "We chowed down before we left our base. But some of the guys might want a bite later on. Do you guys have a PX?"

The RAF man frowned and muttered, "PX? Oh, you mean *canteen!* There's a NAAFI canteen just down the way. You and the other noncoms will be welcome at our

NCO club, of course. I'll take you over, as soon as you assign your men to their new quarters and all that."

Conti said, "Thanks. We'll get our gear inside. Do you have any idea where I can find Captain Evans?"

"He's left the base. Said he was driving into Norwich with Flight Leader Cunningham. He, ah, said I was to tell you your unit's confined to the base until further notice."

Conti nodded and said, "It figures." Then he turned to the trucks and shouted, "Everybody out! Get your gear inside that hut and pick yourselves a place to flop. Yellowpony! Front and center!"

As the men climbed or jumped down from the trucks, a tall lean Amerind separated himself from the others and came over to ask sullenly, "What do you want, Conti?"

Yellowpony was a buck sergeant. Conti outranked him by two stripes, and it was obvious the Amerind thought it was a grave mistake on the Army's part. Conti said, "Get a detail together and unload the special equipment off that last truck. You'd better pile it across the road for now. I'll find out where the captain wants us to store it when he gets back. We'd better put a guard on it too. Some of that stuff goes boom."

Yellowpony said, "I'll do it as soon as I get my own stuff inside and pick out my bed."

Conti shook his head and replied, "No you won't. You'll do what I tell you to do, when I tell you to do it. You got that loud and clear, Chief?"

Yellowpony's eyes narrowed thoughtfully. Then he shrugged and said, "Anything you say, Junior," and turned away with a muttered remark about brown-nosed Italian bastards that Conti chose not to hear.

The flight sergeant pretended he hadn't heard either. The Yank platoon sergeant was quite young and slightly built. His sharply chiseled features were masculine enough, but he didn't look like he was old enough to shave every morning yet.

As if he'd guessed what the older noncom was thinking, Conti smiled and said, "Yellowpony has a hard-on for me because he used to outrank me. But the chief's all right. We jumped in Sicily together and the guy knows how to soldier, when he has to."

"You've already seen combat?" asked the Englishman, frowning. The bloke looked like an effing schoolboy!

Conti said, "Yeah, I've been around the block. Most of these guys have at least one combat jump under their belt. The captain picked us out of a dozen different outfits for this special detail.

A burly trooper came over with a duffel bag to ask, "Where do you want this, Junior?" and Conti said, "Put my stuff by the bunk near the door, Murph."

The trooper nodded and limped toward the hut with Conti's belongings. The flight sergeant sniffed and said, "Your men seem a bit cheeky, don't they, sergeant?"

Conti shrugged and explained, "They haven't got used to the idea yet. The platoon sergeant I replaced was a big tough-looking bastard they called The War Lord. One of those guys who don't look comfortable unless they're picking their teeth with barbed wire and firing a .50 from the hip at the same time."

"I understand your problem. But do you really think you ought to let them call you Junior?"

Conti laughed and said, "Listen. It's better than some of the things they *used* to call me. I draw the line at Dago motherfucker. But it's not worth a trip to fist city every time they make a crack about my age. The War Lord gave me some good advice before he turned the outfit over to me. He said he didn't like to be called War Lord either. But that they could call him Shit For Brains as long as they did as they were told. Some of these guys are in pretty good shape. So it's not a very good idea to punch a paratrooper in the mouth unless you really have to."

"Good lord! Do you Yank NCOs really have to brawl

with the other ranks that often?"

"No. But in the troops, you have to look like you're *willing* to. So far I've been lucky. I had to *offer* to step out behind the barracks with a couple of guys. But nobody's taken me up on it yet. The new stripes give me a little edge. Even if I offer to take off my field jacket and forget the stripes, the guys know they're still there and it's just not worth it to them. They won't admit it. But they know I didn't rate these boots and wings by sending away a couple of boxtops and fifty words or less on why I ate Wheaties. So they'd be taking two chances. I just might whip them, and if they whipped me, I just might be chickenshit enough to turn them in for hitting a noncom. You might say it's a Mexican standoff, for now."

Flight Sergeant Wilkins grimaced and said, "I don't envy you. They seem a wild lot, if you ask me. I don't suppose it's true what they say about your paratroopers being recruited from, well, the lower classes in your country?"

Conti laughed and said, "That's German propaganda. Lord Ha-Ha started that story about us guys being pardoned criminals from Alcatraz and Leavenworth. It's a lot of bullshit. There's a waiting list to get into the troops, and they won't take you if you have a broken bone or a criminal record. I don't think a guy who couldn't make an honest living could make it as a trooper. The discipline at Benning was as rough as West Point, and most of the guys from our old neigborhood who went into the rackets when they grew up wouldn't want to work that hard at anything."

The Negro driver from the lead truck came over to say, "I got to get these trucks back to the motor pool, Sarge."

Conti glanced at the few troopers still in sight and said, "We're almost off-loaded, Mac. You' got plenty of time to get back."

"Not without we drives in the blackout," insisted the worried driver. "These crazy Limey roads is rough to drive on in the *daytime*. Bitty two-lane, high-crown roads between all them hedgerows, with crazy Limeys driving at you down the wrong side and fuckin' Jerry bombers lookin' to spot them bitty blue headlights so's they can blow you' ass off!"

Conti laughed and said, "You got something good waiting for you back at the base, huh? You Blue Star Commandos get more ass than we do as it is. It won't hurt you to miss out one fucking night!"

The driver grinned sheepishly and went back to his truck. Conti said, "The quartermasters do all right for themselves with those cigarettes and C-rations. All we've got going for us is chewing gum and silver wings. I wonder how many sets of silver wings I've given away in this war."

Wilkins frowned and said, "If you ask me, it was a mistake to send those black troops over here. Some I've met seem to be decent chaps. But they will muck about with white women, and it's caused a lot of trouble."

Conti said, "Yeah, I heard about the Manchester race riots. Bunch of stupid white guys fighting with a bunch of stupid black guys over a bunch of stupid twenty-bob whores that none of 'em should have touched with Hitler's dick."

"I take it you approve of those blacks bothering our English girls?"

"I don't approve of anybody *bothering* girls. But if the girl's *willing,* what's that to me? There's always enough ass to go around, and if the Army sends these colored guys overseas, what do they *expect* them to sleep with for Christ's sake?"

"I daresay you wouldn't approve if it was *your* sister!"

"Is your sister sleeping with a colored guy?"

"Of course not! Both my sisters are proper girls!"

"Then what are you sweating about? Take it up with

Roosevelt and Churchill. I don't know a guy in our army, black or white, who wouldn't go home tomorrow, if he was asked polite."

Yellowpony came over to say, "We've got the special shit piled over there under a tree, Junior. Who do you want guarding it?"

"You're a squad leader, Chief. You pick out who you want."

"How come *my* squad? What's the matter with one of the other two squads?"

"Not a thing. I just happened to have picked yours."

"We always get the shit details, damn it!"

"My heart bleeds for you. But it's rough in the ETO."

Yellowpony glowered and said, "Boy, if you weren't wearing them fucking stripes . . ."

Conti looked around, saw there was nothing resembling an officer in sight, and started to unzip his jacket, saying, "Any time you think you're big enough, Chief!"

Before Yellowpony could answer, Flight Sergeant Wilkins snapped, "There'll be none of that, lads! Not on *this* base!"

The Amerind glared at the Englishman and snapped, "Who asked for *your* two cents worth, Limey?"

Conti laughed and said, "We'd better drop it for now, Chief. I think he outranks both of us."

Yellowpony shrugged and said, *"Later,* Junior!" and turned away again, muttering to himself in an angry mixture of English and Dakota curse words.

Conti said, "Thanks. I really thought he was going to call my bluff that time. Just let me see how the guys are making out in there, and I'll buy you a beer at the NCO club you were talking about."

Wilkins walked with him toward the Nissen hut, asking, "You say it was all a bluff, sergeant?"

Conti sighed, "Not *all* a bluff. Sooner or later I'm going to have to fight the crazy Indian asshole!"

"I can see that. But he has twenty pounds on you. Do you really think you can handle him?"

Conti shook his head and replied, "No, I've seen Yellowpony fight. I'm not half that good. He's probably going to kick the shit out of me!"

○○○

The meeting was at a private residence near Blackfriar's Hall in Norwich. The oak paneling and blackout curtains sucked the light from the single ceiling fixture so that the men in the room seemed to be meeting in some underground crypt at midnight, although it was still twilight outside.

Dave Evans had brought some photographs with him and Matt Price sat at a table under the ceiling light, morosely staring down at them as the other men in the room waited for his verdict.

Price had shaved and been issued a British warrant officer's uniform. But his hair hung over his eyes, and his shoulders sagged in a most unmilitary manner inside the too large tunic. After a time, a man in RAF blue cleared his throat and asked, "What about it, Mister Price? Is that the sort of plant you worked in back in Spain?"

Price nodded and said, "It's close enough. But I don't see how we're going to get in through all that mucking wire. Jerry has three fence lines about the place, and if

I know Jerry, the middle fence is electrified. He's likely mined the strips between, too."

An American G2 officer said, "Captain Evans here will get you inside the plant. You just have to worry about putting it out of business!"

Price said, "Those catalytic chambers are delicate. If I had time, I could do it right. But just blowing them up means nothing. Jerry could rebuild them and have the plant back in production in a few weeks."

"A few weeks loss in production means a lot of high-octane fuel the Luftwaffe won't have on D-Day," said someone in the room. But Evans raised a hand for silence and asked, "What do you mean about doing it *right,* Mister Price?"

The ex-Communist said, "There's a big difference between real sabotage and knocking down a lot of bricks, captain. Did you ever sugar the car of someone you didn't like?"

"You mean putting sugar in the gas tank? I've never been that mad at anyone. But I know how it works."

Price nodded and said, "You slash a bloke's tires and take a sledge to his car and what does he do? He buys another flaming car. That's what he does. But sugar in the petrol tank is another thing entire. The poor sod goes on *driving* it, as he wonders why he's spending so bloody much for repairs of late."

Someone asked, "What does this sugar business do to a car?"

Price explained, "It gums up the works. The fuel line clogs and has to be cleaned out. The valves stick and have to be reground. The carb needs cleaning every few miles. The bloody car just eats away at the bloke's pocket-book while the mechanics keep trying to make it run. We used to pour battery acid in a Lorry's radiator too. You can repair a lot of radiator leaks before you know what's wrong, and sooner or later, the engine has to be scrapped.

Ruddy hard on the mechanic's hands too!"

Evans nodded and said, "I see what you're getting at. You'd rather tinker with the catalytic process so that it doesn't work right. Is that it?"

Price nodded and said, "Change the mixture of the synthesis gas by getting to the right valves, and you'll drive Jerry crazy with shut downs and repairs. Enrich the gas with oxygen and the carbon monoxide changes to carbon *di*oxide before it catalyzes."

"What would that do?"

"The gas would look and smell like synthesis gas. But it wouldn't liquefy proper. Not unless they changed the catalyst. They'd think they had the temperature set wrong, and Lord knows how long it would take them to figure out what they were doing different. They'd have to shut down and dismantle the chambers to replace the catalyst grids. Then, if they hadn't spotted the oxygen feeding in, the whole thing would start all over. The gas would come out of the retorts, boil around inside the catalytic chambers, and refuse to behave. Wouldn't that be loverly?"

Evans asked, "Where would we get all this extra oxygen?"

"From Jerry, of course. You haven't paid proper attention to the Haber process, Yank. You feed a mix of ox and live steam into the coal beds in the first bloody place. The ox and water hitting the hot coals turn to hydrogen and CO. So there's no free oxygen left in the mix by the time it goes to the catalytic chamber."

"I thought you added oxygen to the producer gas to . . ."

"You thought wrong. Carbon *mon*oxide *burns*. Carbon *di*oxide puts fires *out!* Didn't you learn nothing in chemistry, Yank?"

"Not as much as I thought. That's why I asked for you, Price."

Mollified, the older man explained, "A little ox bled into the mix converts the CO into worthless CO_2. Bleed in a bit too much and it combines with the hydrogen to give you one hell of an explosion! The process is tricky as a Swiss watch and twice as easy to sabotage. If you could give me a few hours on the cracking towers, I could *really* do a job!"

"Negative on the cracking towers. We don't want to break any windows in that hospital next door!"

"Who said anything about breaking windows? I just want to muck about with the valves. If there was a hidden by-pass, feeding wax into the aviation fuel, nobody would notice it at ground level."

Flight Leader Cunningham grinned and said, "I see what you mean! The wax would start to solidify at high altitude and . . . Oh, that's rich, Mister Price. I'm certainly glad you're on *our* side in this bloody war!"

Price said, "I'm not so bloody sure I am. I was promised a commission, and all they gave me was a bloody warrant. Nobody's told me how we're supposed to get away from that perishing place either!"

Someone said, "Warrant officer was the best we could do, in view of your, ah, past activities, Mister Price."

But Price insisted, "Stuff the rank. It's my *arse* I'm worried most about at the moment! I mean, I keep asking how we get out and so far, nobody seems to know!"

Dave Evans had his own reservations. But he said, "We're working on that, Mister Price. Right now, we're supposed to be planning our best moves if and when we get *to* the target!"

"You say you have a platoon? I thought a captain led a full company."

"I am a company commander, or rather, I was until I signed up for this mission. We haven't the transport for more than thirty men or so."

Price shook his head and said, "Thirty men ain't near enough. Jerry must have at least a company of guards at the damned concentration camp. If they're holding allied

PWs in the hospital, they'll have guards posted there too!"

The G2 man said, "There's one company of SS guards, period. They're based at the camp and supply guards to the entire area."

"What about the hydrogenation plant itself?"

"Handful of security men from the Todt Administration. They act as gate guards and night watchmen. No heavy weapons. If they get in trouble, they're supposed to call the SS for help."

Evans added, "We have the telephone wires mapped. They go down before anything else."

Price shrugged and said, "Look, I don't care about the details of getting *in*. I want to know how we get *out!*"

"We'll get you in *and* out," promised Evans, even as he wondered how he intended to manage such a thing. The Tall General had been rather vague about that part. But there *had* to be *some* plan! They wouldn't throw thirty men away like used Kleenex tissues, would they?

As if to change the subject, the G2 man said, "This sabotage stuff sounds pretty tricky. As I understand it, you drop into the woods a few miles from the target and . . ."

"Negative on woods!" cut in Evans. "Jump into second growth timber at night and you'll lose half the men before they reach the ground! We have the Kellermann farm picked as the DZ. It's an isolated dairy farm. Open pasture for the most part. No phone lines visible in any of the photo recon shots. The Kellermann family has two sons serving on the eastern front. Two Russian slave laborers work the dairy herd for the old man and his wife. The first stick takes the farmhouse and secures the area. We figure we can recruit the two Russians to help us."

"And if you can't?" asked Price.

"We kill them," said Evans bleakly.

"What about the German family?"

"We'll have to wing it. If they're alone when we drop

in on them, we may be able to hold them without anyone getting hurt. If we have to take them out, we have to take them out. Old man Kellermann's supposed to be a veteran of the last war. He might be reasonable. He might want to go down waving the flag. Either way, we take and secure the farm for a base."

"And once we have a base on the ground?"

"We get you into the hydrogenation plant. We'll reconnoiter before we commit ourselves. It may be possible to sneak in on the QT. We may have to move in shooting from the hip. You've told us what you can do if we sneak you in. So, what do you suggest if we can't be subtle, Mister Price?"

Price sighed and asked, "Do I have primacord to work with?"

"Sure. Primacord, satchel charges, gelatinite, you name it."

"I'll use primacord then. Wrap as many pipes as I can while your lot keep Jerry off. Then place some satchel charges between the retort and catalytic chamber, light the bloody fuses, and run like bloody hell! You still haven't told me where we run *to*, Yank!"

"If we get you in, we get you out. You let us worry about that. The thing is, you're sure you can put the plant out of production, one way or the other."

"I keep telling you I can," insisted Price. "And you keep telling me that you're getting us out of there afterwards. But you don't seem to want to tell me *how*, Yank!"

"It's classified," said Evans, wondering why he hadn't thought of that before. This so-called expert they'd saddled him with seemed pretty edgy. He had to keep him on the ball somehow, until he figured out, himself, how the fuck any of them were coming out of this mission alive. Aloud, he said, "We've got to get back to the air base, Mister Price. We've only got a little more than a day to teach you the rudiments of parachuting out of a Mosquito at treetop level."

Price shot him a worried look, and he knew he'd gotten the man's mind off the *distant* future. He smiled and said, "It's not as rugged as it sounds. We jump with static lines. The whole thing's automatic. We only have to teach you how to come down limp and spill your chute. Anyone can learn it in a few hours."

Flight Leader Cunningham frowned and started to speak. But Evans caught his eye, and he choked back what he'd begun to say about not having any static lines in the bombers they were using. He assumed, correctly, that Evans would explain the matter to Price before they boarded.

One of the officers in the room glanced pointedly at his wrist and said, "I'll let you fellows work out the details. I have a few calls to make."

He left the room and went downstairs. He left the building and crossed the street to a public telephone booth. He called a certain number and disguised his voice as he murmured into the phone, "Your information about the turncoat was correct, comrade. I just left a meeting he attended."

A voice on the other end of the line said, "You must liquedate Price at once. If you have to drop your cover to do it, make for the embassy and we will see to a new identity for you."

The man in the booth, who looked very much like an American officer who'd never returned from a three-day pass in the lake district, said, "Impossible, comrade."

The man on the other end of the line said, "Bah, you play chess when name of the game is checkers! I tell you we have orders about that traitor. Why can't you get him tonight?"

"He is on his way to a British airdrome with several officers. If it was broad daylight, I could pick him off from across the street. In this light, that is impossible."

"Can you follow him?"

"No. But I know where he's going. He's going on a joint Anglo-American mission into Germany!"

"You know details of this mission, comrade?"

"Of course. I told you I attended the meeting. They still think I'm Lieutenant Chambers of the CIC."

There was a long silence. Then the voice said, "You had better report to embassy at once. Our comrades will want to know all about this business!"

The man in the booth glanced over his shoulder and murmured, "If I just drop out of sight, they may suspect something. My cover's not good enough to stand up under a thorough investigation and . . ."

"You will catch next train for London and let us worry about what British and Americans suspect. That is an *order*, comrade!"

The man in the booth said, "I'm on my way. But they're going to find out I wasn't Chambers. If they really start looking for Chambers, they're going to end up dragging Lake Buttermere and . . ."

"And they'll decide you were German spy," laughed the voice at the other end. "What do we care what they suspect dirty Germans of, comrade? After all, it's not as if they have any reason to suspect *us*, is there?"

The spy in the phone booth chuckled and, in restored good humor, replied, "Of course not, comrade. Everybody knows that the Soviet Union is on the same side as the so-called Allies!"

○○

The man from the US State Department was pacing nervously outside the Tall General's door. He was out of cigarettes and he didn't like the Tall General. Nobody in State liked the Tall General since he'd taken it in his head to negotiate with the enemy on his own that time in North Africa. They said he drank and screwed around a lot. That was the trouble with soldiers. They had no discipline.

An attractive, somewhat blowzy WAC officer came out of the Tall General's office and said, "The general can see you now, Mister Lowell."

The man from State glanced pointedly at his watch and nodded grimly. Then he went inside to beard the lion in its den. He got right to the point by saying, "We just heard about your airborne attack on Vogelbach, general. What's this nonsense about paratroopers invading Switzerland, for God's sake?"

The Tall General looked innocent and replied, "I don't know what you're talking about, Lowell. No troops under *my* command have ever been ordered to violate Swiss neutrality!"

"Let's not bullshit each other, general. State has its own reliable sources and we know you're out to destroy that coal hydrogenation plant at Vogelbach. I've already been to RAF headquarters and the damned British are being pigheaded about it too!"

The Tall General smiled and said, "The RAF's not pigheaded, Lowell. They just don't want to see all those FW-190s buzzing around in their windshields on D-Day. You see, *fighting* a war gives a guy a certain perspective you guys at State seem to miss at times!"

Lowell frowned and snapped, "Let's not be handing out that heroic bullshit, general! I could tell you some war stories that would curl your hair. You're a soldier who sits behind a desk. I'm a civilian who's spent more time behind enemy lines than you have in the chow line!"

"Okay. You're one of Dulles's boys and you've been running around pissing in German gas tanks or something. So we both deserve a medal, and I'm still going to knock that purple-pissing Nazi refinery out this weekend. What's it to State?"

"The diplomatic flap it's going to cause! We don't care how many hydrogenation plants you guys knock out. But you can't order a platoon of US paratroopers to cross the Swiss border. They're still yelling at us about those damned planes that bombed a Swiss border town by mistake last year!"

The Tall General said, "I know Swiss policy. They've interned over a hundred British, American, and German flyers who strayed into their territory. But it's my understanding the Swiss have treated all of them very hospitably. The internees have been put up at Swiss hotels and given military paroles. They report in to the Swiss authorities from time to time, but walk around Zurich as free as big-ass birds. Our guys get their pay and mail from home as if they were here in England. They can't come home until the war is over. But they can buy all the chocolate they want and some of them have married Swiss girls. It's a pretty good deal. I understand more than one flyboy has managed to lose himself over Switzerland on purpose and . . ."

"Accidents are one thing. *Ordering* men to cross the border is another. We can't let you do it, general!"

"Now, who said anything about my ordering any such thing, Mister Lowell? I'll show you a copy of my orders, if you like. You won't find Switzerland mentioned in any orders issued by *this* office!"

Lowell snorted and asked, "Come on, how are those men supposed to get away after they knock out that plant? There's no place for them to *go* but Switzerland, damn it!"

"Oh, I don't know. They might be able to fight their way across Occupied France to the channel, and they've got an R-300 pack. They might radio for help and the royal commandos could meet them on some deserted stretch of beach, or they could steal a German submarine, or . . ."

"Don't hand me that shit, general! When the Germans find out thirty US paratroopers are wandering around on the Upper Rhine, they'll be chasing them with a division of mountain troops and a couple of Luftwaffe squadrons! The only chance those poor kids have is a run for the Swiss frontier and you know it!"

The Tall General reached for a cigar and bit the end off it before he said mildly, "Gee, I hadn't thought of that. I guess they might decide to run for Switzerland at that. But I promise you they have no such instructions, Mister Lowell."

"Will you issue a direct order that they're *not* to cross the Swiss frontier under any circumstances, general?"

"I'm not sure I can. Would the Eighth Air Force go

along with such an order, Mister Lowell?"

"What are you talking about? What has the Eighth Air Force got to do with this madness?"

"They've been telling flyers shot down over Germany what a peachy-keen place Switzerland is, compared to a German stalag. And, like I said, there's a whole shithouse full of American bomber crews sweating out the end of the war in the Alps."

"Look, it's not the same thing. The Swiss frontier guards will swallow an occasional refugee crossing over from Germany. But an airborne invasion is something else, damn it!"

"They'll probably be pretty browned off, huh?"

"You can bet your ass they will! They might, repeat, *might* not shoot them. But they're going to let out a diplomatic scream that'll be heard in the White House, and more important, they might close the border permanently to all future refugees!"

"Gee, I hadn't thought of that! I guess, when we cross the Rhine this summer, the poor purple-pissing Nazis will have no place to run to, huh?"

"You'll never cross the Rhine this year and you know it!"

"Okay. So they won't have any place to go in '45. But we're going to knock out that synthetic fuel plant in the meantime, and once my kids do it, I don't give a fuck *where* they run to!"

"You have to order them to stay away from the Swiss frontier."

"I do? I'll tell you what, Mister Lowell, you just run up to Eighth Air Force headquarters and get them to issue such an order to their flyboys, and I'll issue the same order to my troops."

"Don't be ridiculous! Even if I could get them to issue such an order, I'd never be able to get back to you before your men took off on this crazy mission of yours!"

The Tall General reached for a desk lighter and lit his cigar. He blew a cloud of Havana Perfecto in the other man's face and marveled, "Gee, I never thought of that!"

oo

Dave Evans introduced Matt Price to Sergeant Conti and said, "Pete, I want you to issue Mister Price a .45 and a parachute. Do you know how to use a .45, Mister Price?"

Price nodded and said, "Yes. But I wish I knew how to use a perishing parachute!"

Evans smiled at Conti and said, "There's a gym over by the service club, Pete. Rig up some sort of a platform and show Mister Price how to land. I'll be with him to spill his chute when we hit the ground. So just concentrate on teaching him to save his ankles. Have the men had any dry runs in the planes we're using tonight?"

Conti nodded. But his face was clouded as he said, "Some of the guys were asking about those Mosquitos, captain. They're a lot smaller than any C-47, and well, they seem to be made out of *wood!*"

"Plywood," nodded Evans. "The De Haviland people seem to like to build their airframes the old-fashioned way. But Miss Mosquito's a good kite, Pete. She's got the

45

speed of a fighter. Range and payload of our B-17. The wood frame is an added bonus nobody was thinking about when they designed her."

"That piano box fuselage has an *advantage,* sir?"

"Right. A wooden airframe doesn't have a radar echo. Do I have to draw you a picture, Pete?"

Conti grinned and asked, "Do you mean the Krauts can't see us on their radar screens, sir?"

"That's right. That's why the British have been using Miss Mosquito as everything from a bomber to a night fighter. You might spread that around among the men. We'll move like spit on a hot stove, and even if the Krauts spot us, they haven't a fighter that can catch up with the hot kites we'll be riding in!"

Conti nodded and said, "I'll tell them, sir. It might help. Some of the guys were bitching about not having a static line too."

Evans ignored the worried look Price threw him and said, "You're all qualified for a free jump and it's better this way. We're going to be jammed like sardines in those three planes, and diving out the bomb-bay doors that way, it's better that each man pulls his own rip cord."

Price gasped, "Hoy! You told me my ruddy parachute would open automatically, Yank!"

Evans said, "We're jumping together, Mister Price. I'll have a length of static line tied to your chute. I'll pull the plug for you in plenty of time. The others have to count to four."

Conti frowned and asked, *"Four?* Don't you mean *ten,* sir?"

"Not at the speed and altitude we'll be dropping from, Pete. I want us all to come down in the same neighborhood, and there are a lot of fir trees in the area of that farm. Have you picked a detail to secure the farmstead yet?"

"I figured I'd do it myself, sir."

"I'm going to need you, and the R-300 with me. What's the matter with Yellowpony? His stick could hit the farmhouses, couldn't they?"

Conti looked uncomfortable and Evans insisted, "Why not? Yellowpony jumped in Sicily and he's supposed to be a hell of a soldier."

"He is, sir. But, well, I thought you wanted those civilians taken *alive,* captain."

"I do if it can be done that way. Don't you think Yellowpony can do it, Pete?"

"He could if he *wanted* to, captain. But Yellowpony might not want to. I mean, the chief's a good old boy in a fire fight. But in Sicily, he killed people a lot."

"You mean he's a sadist?"

"Nossir, I wouldn't call him a sadist. He doesn't want to *hurt* anybody. He just wants to *kill* them! Chief lost some buddies in Sicily, and I don't think he ever cared that much about the Geneva Conventions in the first place."

"What about Sergeant Compton's stick?"

"Compton's all right, sir. He's a quiet guy who does as he's told. I'll go over it again with Compton and tell him to make straight for the farmhouses while Yellowpony sets up a perimeter at the tree line. My guys can gather up the gear and . . . I'm sorry, sir. I didn't mean to tell you how to run your show."

Evans smiled and said, "You're doing fine, Pete. I picked you for the job because I knew you could think on your feet. Any officer who thinks he can run the whole show is asking for a lot of Purple Hearts. I'm counting on you noncoms to worry about the details. Mister Price and I have enough other things to worry about, eh, Mister Price?"

"I think I'm going to shoot myself and save Jerry the

trouble," said Price, and Evans laughed. The sabotage expert had been grousing ever since they'd met. But he was all right. They'd told Evans about some of the crazy things he'd done in the past, and the guy had more hair on his chest than he admitted to.

Trooper Muprhy came over to them, saluted, and said, "There's a lady to see you, captain."

"A lady? To see me?"

"Yessir. WAC lieutenant. She's waiting in your quarters with a message from headquarters."

Evans left Price with the sergeant and crossed the parade ground with trooper Murphy. An American staff car was parked in front of the BOQ, and a bored-looking driver lounged against a fender, smoking a cigarette. He palmed the smoke and saluted as Evans approached and said, "Lieutenant Mason is in your room, captain. The RAF orderly said she could use your john and wait for you there."

Evans went inside and found the door to his room ajar. He opened it and saw the Tall General's secretary sitting on his bunk. She'd taken off her tunic and thrown it over a chair with her hat. She didn't rise as he entered, but smiled and asked, "Have you a cigarette, Dave? This rationing is really getting me down, and Limey butts are half a crown a pack. That's nearly fifty cents, for Pete's sake! Can you imagine anyone paying fifty cents for a pack of cigarettes?"

Evans took out a half-empty pack of Pall Malls and offered it to her, saying, "Keep the pack. I've got another and I don't figure to be smoking much tonight."

She took the cigarettes, waited until he'd offered her a light, and said, "That's what I came to see you about. I have a few last minute, uh, suggestions."

He nodded and she said, "Close the door and lock it. This is off the record. Officially, I'm not here."

Evans shut the door and threw the barrel bolt. Then he turned and asked, "What's this all about, lieutenant?"

"Call me Barbara, Dave. My friends all call me Barbara and this is a friendly visit. If you repeat what I'm about to tell you, I'll deny every word of it, and the general will be very annoyed with you."

He nodded, and the woman patted the gray wool at her side, saying, "Sit down. We've got to get a few things straight before you and your men take off."

Evans joined her on the bed, suddenly aware of the perfume and the seductive smell of shampooed hair. She patted his knee and said, "We've been catching a lot of flack from State. They don't mind what you're trying to do. But the mothers seem to want to see you killed doing it. You remember the general saying he'd get around to your escape plans before you took off?"

Evans nodded and said, "Yeah. I've been wondering if he planned to have a Greyhound bus waiting for us after we knocked out the refinery. I take it there *is* some way out of there for us?"

"You take it wrong, Dave. There isn't any way for you to get your men out, officially."

"What do you mean? What are we supposed to do? Those kids are *counting* on me, uh, Barbara!"

She took his hand, squeezed it, and said, "Let's not get our bowels in an uproar, honey! I said *officially*, remember?"

"Right. So what's the score?"

"Switzerland. Once you take care of that Nazi refinery, you're on your own. But the Swiss frontier is only a few miles away and there's plenty of cover. If you move at night, you can be over the border and well inside Cuckoo Clock Land before the sun comes up. We're cutting orders forbidding you to do it. But the orders won't get here before you take off."

Evans frowned and said, "Have the Swiss agreed to send us home, then?"

She held his hand in her lap and said, "The Swiss don't know you're coming. But they won't hurt you. They'll disarm you and take you to Zurich for a stern lecture on neutrality. Then they'll assign quarters to you and your men and stuff you full of cheese and chocolate. It's really wild in Zurich. You see GIs and Limeys and Krauts wandering around in all the bars. They say the Krauts salute our officers when they pass them on the street. You and your guys will have a lot to write home about."

"I can't order my men into internment! They'll be held there until the end of the war!"

"So what? The war will be over by Christmas! All you'll be missing is a chance to die on D-Day, Dave! You make this one jump, and for you, the war is over. You'll get your pay and promotion just as if you never left England. I don't know how you feel about medals. But we're going to give you some of those too. Ike has some idea about sending men home at the end of the war according to how many medals they have. So we've been collecting them a lot at headquarters. Anyway, about this Swiss angle . . ."

"No officer can order his men to surrender! It's the only direct order any soldier is free to disobey!"

She shrugged and said, "Okay. So they can refuse to follow you and take their chances with the whole German army. Would that make any sense, Dave?"

"No. But neither would volunteering to be captured by the Swiss, damn it! You can tell the general he has to do better than that, Barbara. My men and I aren't about to take off on any such mission!"

"Oh, are you ever *wrong,* honey! The mission is set for tonight. Over and out."

"Suppose I put it to them? Suppose I put it to a vote?"

"What are you talking about? Since when did anybody

get to vote in this man's army? They're going, Dave. With or without you, they're going."

"Suppose I refuse to lead them?"

"We have to find another officer in one hell of a hurry. But we'll find one. We can always find one, Dave. The army is full of eager-beaver paratroopers!"

Evans fell silent as he tried to gather his thoughts. The woman massaged his hand deeper into her lap and said, "You don't want a Section Eight, do you, honey?"

Evans blinked in surprise and said, "You mean, if I spill the beans I get sent home as a psycho, for God's sake?"

She nodded and said, "Yes, and your men would be jumping with someone else. Someone who might not know what he was doing. Is that what you want, Dave?"

"If you were a man, right now, I'd belt you in the mouth!"

Barbara dimpled and said, "I know. That's why they gave this shit detail to a woman."

He didn't answer for a time. Then he shrugged and said, "I guess I have no choice, huh?"

"No choice at all, honey. It's rough in the ETO."

She waited until she saw he'd run out of things to say. Then she lay back on the bed, holding his hand in place between her thighs as she murmured, "I know how you feel, Dave. I wish there was some way I could make it up to you."

He shrugged dully and said, "You can tell the son of a bitch I'll do it. But if I ever meet him after the war . . ."

She said, "Dave. I don't have to be back until this evening. I have the whole afternoon and . . ."

He became aware of what she was doing with his hand and frowned. Cautiously he asked, "Do you mean that the way I think you mean it, lieutenant?"

She purred, "Only if you promise to use a rubber. I brought some along, just in case."

Dave Evans got to his feet and pulled down the blackout curtain, muttering, "It's nice to know my men and I aren't the only people getting fucked in this man's army!"

A German officer sat in a bombproof office under Berlin reading a sheaf of photostated memos typed on a British machine. The light was bad and the photostats were out of focus. The German's eyes hurt and he knew he had to get a new prescription for his reading glasses. So much reading there was in this stupid job he had. So much reading and so few facts and, always, the dry taste of fear in one's mouth. The fear that somehow one had missed a pattern or, worse yet, seen a pattern where there was none!

The steel door slid open, and a younger man in a black leather raincoat came in. He said, "One of our informants just overheard something in a Norwich pub, Herr Oberst."

The colonel lowered the sheaf he'd been reading through and said, "Someone is always hearing something in a British pub. The damned British talk even more than they drink. But they seldom say anything. What was it this time?"

"A mission, Herr Oberst. A crewman on a British

Mosquito was overheard talking about a secret mission this very night!"

"Norwich is in East Anglia. The British and American bombers *come* from East Anglia. They are on a secret mission every day and night. Their last secret mission did something to the lights in here. Turn over your information to General Galland's people and let the Luftwaffe Fighter Command worry about it!"

"It's not that simple, Herr Oberst. Our informant overheard them talking about a synthetic fuel refinery!"

"So? They intend to bomb another hydrogenation plant. That is hardly news. They've been bombing the damned things all winter! I happen to know we have a screen of ME-110s flying high-altitude radar patrols every night. Those damned Mosquitos are hard to spot on a radar-scope. But that's not our problem. Pass your information on to the Luftwaffe and forget it."

"Herr Oberst," the other insisted, "this is not to be a bombing mission. There was a mention of paratroopers."

"Paratroopers? Jumping out of Mosquitos? That's insane. And why would they be sending in paratroopers so early? We know D-Day won't come before July at the earliest. They have to wait for calm water in the English Channel. Your information has to be a mistake. Some Englishman was just talking big for the others to hear."

The man in the raincoat nodded and started to leave. The colonel said, "Wait," and took off his glasses. He rubbed his eyes and muttered, "You'd better follow up on it. Get in touch with our people in England and ask them to see what they can find out about this crazy business."

ooo

Later, though the flight seemed to take a million years, none of the survivors would remember much about the trip but the discomfort. The overloaded Mosquitos took off at midnight, their twin Merlins pulling them through the thick, low-altitude night air at fighter speed. It was said the Lockheed P-38 could give a Mosquito a run for its money. If this was true, the P-38 was the only other twin engine plane in the war that could.

Back in the gutted fuselages, the men of Operation Octane were packed like rush-hour commuters in a New York subway train. There hadn't been enough breathing space for any of them to carry his reserve chute. But, as Sergeant Conti cheerfully observed, you didn't need a reserve at treetop level.

There were no windows. A single light had been jury-rigged on the forward bulkhead. In a regular transport, there was a series of jump lights that told you when it was time to leave. The RAF crews not knowing the form, a loudspeaker had been installed to give the signals verbally, and from time to time, the pilot told them where they were. The names of French towns meant nothing to the passengers crowded in the plywood tube to his rear. But it was reassuring to know they were making progress. The captain, Price, and Sergeant Conti were more or less visible in the dim light near the bomb bay. The stick behind them faded back into the darkness like ghostly minstrel-show comics. Each of them had blacked his face with burnt cork and their jump suits had been daubed with black shoe polish. Dog tags were wrapped in friction tape to keep them from clinking, and wool socks had been pulled on over the jump boots. Nobody wore a helmet. Helmets make a hell of a noise against fir trees, and if they did it right, nobody was going to lob any mortar rounds at their heads anyway.

They were traveling light. So each man carried a skeletonized carbine instead of a Thompson. The carbines could fire full auto if they had to. But they were set on single fire. Carbine ammo was light. But they could only carry so much, and it would have to last them the rest of the war. In addition to his carbine and folding jump knife, each man had a US navy survival knife on his right boot. The army had learned about this particular navy issue from the marines and, like the eight-inch prox fuse shell, adopted it for its own. The US navy survival knife had been designed to be an all-around tool for navy pilots landing in a jungle. Its heavy hilt could be used as a hammer or a club. Its short-wicked blade could cut through timber bamboo, or a human spinal column, without losing its edge. It was the best fighting knife that money could buy, and the men had been trained to use it. They'd practiced on cabbages. Cutting a human throat was said to feel very much like slicing through a cabbage. Nobody was too clear about just who'd made the discovery.

Dave Evans heard strange sounds above the roar of the engines and craned his head around at Sergeant Conti to shout, "What?" and the baby-faced sergeant looked away sheepishly. Pete Conti had a secret vice. He sang in the shower and whenever he was near a roaring engine. In a C-47, you could sing all you wanted and nobody would hear you. The engines were louder in this plane. But they were packed in too tight for privacy. He couldn't sing on this mission. The guys would laugh at him.

The intercom blared something that sounded very much like, "Oh, shit!" and Evans nudged Price to shout, "What was that?"

"He said shit!" shouted Price above the engine's roar. After a time the navigator crawled back to shout, "We just lost a plane. MacTavish flew into the fucking barrage-balloon cable over that last town back there. Skipper wants to know if we abort!"

Evans swallowed the green taste in his mouth as he tried to remember which plane MacTavish had been piloting. He muttered, "Christ! That was Yellowpony's stick!" and added, in a louder voice, "Negative! Tell 'em up front to keep going!"

The navigator vanished from view, and Evans reached around to shake Conti, shouting, "Compton secures the farmhouses, right?"

"Yessir. What was that about the other plane? I couldn't hear."

"Yellowpony's people bought the farm. Take half your men to the tree line when we land. Leave at least four with me and I'll bring in the gear. You're going to be spread too thin if you try for a full perimeter. Just secure the approaches from the main road and have a couple patrolling the woods in a circle. Got that, sergeant?"

Conti nodded as Evans studied his face. The kid was tougher than he looked, or a good poker player. Military maxim has it that the cracking point is one-third casualties, and they'd just lost a third of their force. Conti didn't look happy about it. But he wasn't wetting his pants either. The guy's 201 file had been right, it seemed. Conti had been this route before.

What about the others? How would the other men react to what had happened? Some of them were green. This was Sergeant Compton's first combat jump, and there was no way to talk to him in that other plane. The other pilot would have told them what happened by now. What if Compton ordered his pilot to turn back? The RAF guys must be as shaken as he was. They'd known MacTavish as a friend and comrade. What if, when he got to the DZ, there was nobody here but us chickens?

"Our pilot will tell us," he said aloud, unheard above the engines' roar. He nodded and said, "Compton's only a noncom. He can't order an abort. Nobody can order an abort but me!"

A small voice inside him asked, "So, what are you *waiting* for, you jerk?"

○○○

The room in London was brightly lit and garishly furnished. Red velvet drapes hung over the blackout curtains, and Joseph Stalin stared down from a baroque gilt frame at the heavyset man playing chess with himself at the ornate rosewood desk. There was another man in the room. But he hadn't been invited to join the game. Master chessmen find it painful to match their skills against lesser mortals.

The chessmaster moved a pawn and said, "So the traitor, Price, will be landing in Germany at any minute, da?"

The other man nodded and said, "Yes. We have the whole plan here. The Americans are careless about the carbons they throw in waste baskets, comrade."

The chessmaster said, "Is delicate situation we have on our hands, isn't it?"

The other nodded and said, "Our orders on Price are quite clear. The man was Moscow trained, and when this war is over, someone is sure to listen to his rantings. You know, of course, about the book he tried to publish in America?"

The chessmaster shrugged and said, "I read it. Was very badly written. I don't blame American publishers for turning it down."

"The man is uneducated and his book was very tedious. But also very *accurate,* comrade! He named too many names and has too many facts about the way we operate. Someday, when the British and Americans grow up, they may take a second look at that mad turncoat's manuscript. He has to be liquidated. Our orders are quite clear about ex-Comrade Price!"

"I know. But damned war has complicated matters. We have other orders too. Orders to help our so-called allies against Nazi beast. You had your chance at Price when we traced him to that merchant ship. But you failed, comrade. It wasn't Price who went overboard that night. Was our East Indian comrade who went for midnight swim. You have never explained how that could have happened, comrade."

"How does one explain the nine lives of a cat? Price is an old party man. He knows our methods, and the British prison system seems to have taught him a few more tricks. He has the cunning of a Cockney wharf rat to go with what we taught him in Moscow."

The chessmaster moved another pawn and chided, "Accuracy, comrade, *accuracy.* Price is not Cockney. Was born in Wales and raised in Birmingham. His people were colliers, and he worked way through industrial school before we recruited him. You pigeonhole our enemies so quickly. Mathew Price is more than meets the eye. That is why he's still alive, as well as the reason we must put end to his checkered career."

"He's going to be in Switzerland soon. Do I cable the Zurich office?"

"Not so fast, comrade. The Swiss are tidy people. They

ask all sorts of questions when people die in Switzerland. I think would be much better if *Germans* killed him for us. Price has certain reputation with the Fascists. Once they know who they've captured, they'll want to discuss couple of things he did to their friends in Spain."

He moved another pawn and nodded, asking, "Who do we have that can see that Germans learn about this mission?"

"One of our men has been sleeping with a German agent who thinks she's Mata Hari. He says she has a wireless set in her attic. She's not very good in bed. But she's been sending a lot of useless information we've been feeding her to the Nazis."

"Tell our comrade about the Anglo-American strike on Fabrik Vogelbach and ask him to sacrifice himself once more for his country. Who is he pretending to be, anyway?"

"An American soldier. He's a *real* American soldier by the way. He was working in Cleveland when they drafted him. I'll tell him to leave early so he can get right to her wireless."

The chessmaster sighed and said, "You *must* learn not to jump gun this way, comrade. You know as well as I that Price is very good saboteur. We may be *using* Germans. But we hardly owe them any *favors!*"

"I'm not sure I follow you, comrade."

"Is because you are man of action. Too much action in too much of hurry. I don't want Germans to know Price is behind their lines until *after* hydrogenation plant is blown up! That new Panther tank Nazis have has been causing us a lot of trouble in field. We don't want Nazis to have fuel any more than our so-called allies do!"

"I see what you mean, comrade. We give Operation Octane a head start before we let the Nazis know about it."

"Of course. If I know Price, he'll need less than day to do job on that German plant. If we time it just so, Nazis will cut whole mission off before they reach the Swiss frontier. I think our American soldier should pay call on his Nazi sweetheart and tell her about mission. But, then he must keep her from sending before evening. Let him take her out and how do they say, crawl in pubs until closing time?

"Americans will lay low during day, hit plant and run for it as soon as it gets dark. By then, Nazis will have started moving in their patrols, and since they'll know where paratroopers are going . . . Damn, I should have sacrificed knight two moves back!"

The other man grinned and said, "I like the plan, comrade. Price will never get away this time. But what do you think the Germans will do to the Americans?"

The chessmaster shrugged and said, "What does it matter? If a few Americans die in this war, we won't have to fight them in next!"

◦◦◦

The roar of engines rattled the windows and awoke Horst Kellermann from a vaguely unpleasant dream. He stared up in the darkness for a time as the sounds faded, trying to remember the dream and wondering why some fool was flying so low. Didn't he know there were hills all around this valley?

A dog was barking outside. Poor Kaiser was upset about all that noise. The hound was old and beginning to snap. One of these days he'd have to take the poor old beast out behind the barn and shoot it. Momma had asked him to, more than once. But he kept putting it off. Karl had raised Der Kaiser from a pup and . . .

The woman laying at his side nudged him under the quilt and murmured, "What was that noise, Poppa?"

Kellermann said, "A low-flying plane, momma. Go back to sleep."

"Der Kaiser is barking about something. Do you suppose the deer could be getting into my garden again?"

"The plane woke him up. There are no deer in your

garden. That noise would have frightened them into the next valley by now if they *were* trying to get in. Sleep, momma. We have a big day ahead of us."

The two of them fell silent for a time. Then the woman insisted, "Kaiser is still barking. There's somebody out there, poppa!"

"One of the Russians, momma. The plane must have awakened him and he's gone to the outhouse. Der Kaiser has never accepted the Russians and he always barks at them."

"I don't know why they sent those Russians to us, poppa. We had two fine sons to work this farm in the first place. Why did they have to take my babies and give me Russians? I liked it better the other way."

Kellermann sighed, put an arm around his wife, and said, "Lay your head on my shoulder, little treasure, and we can talk about such things in the morning."

The woman snuggled closer to her husband and tried not to think about little Karl in those ridiculous stovepipe boots. It wasn't so bad they'd taken Wolfgang. Wolfgang was big and strong, like poppa. She knew her Wolfgang had been the toughest boy at the gymnasium and that it was an honor to be chosen for the SS. But Karl was so young and scrawny to be a soldier on the eastern front. They should have left him here with his momma and poppa. He wasn't old enough to be so far from home, and he wrote to her so seldom.

She started to cry and her husband patted her, saying, "Sleep, momma. We have to be up early. The Russians and I are spreading manure on the north pasture in the morning, and those Ivans eat like horses. I am counting on you for a hearty breakfast and . . .

"Poppa," she cut in, "there is somebody *out* there!"

"Der Kaiser has stopped barking."

"Yes. But I don't like the way he stopped, poppa. He stopped in the *middle* of a bark. He's never stopped barking like that before. Always Der Kaiser's barking runs down, like a top. I think you'd better have a look!"

Horst Kellermann sighed and sat up in bed. There was no use talking to momma when she got this way. She was a village girl, and in twenty years, she'd never gotten used to the small country noises of an isolated farmstead. He swung his feet to the floor, went to the window, and opened it. He leaned his head out and shouted, "All right, you ghosts! Back to the graveyard you go!"

Then he came back to the bed, got in it, and said, "There. Are you satisfied?"

"Poppa! There's something on the stairs!"

"Don't be silly, momma. The Russians never come in the house without knocking, and besides, it's quiet as a tomb out there!"

"You don't hear so well as I, poppa. I tell you something was on the stairs just now, and ach, Gott! It's right outside the door!"

Kellermann put an arm around her again and laughed, "It must be grandpa. You used to hear him around the house after he passed away, remember?"

He ran his free hand down her flank and added slyly, "As long as we can't sleep, old woman, I'd better give you something to think about, eh?"

"Stop that, you old fool! I don't want to make love at a time like this! Get your hand away from there! We're about to be murdered in our bed and all you can think of is feeling me up!"

"Better I should feel up someone else? Come on, little treasure. There may be snow on our roof tops. But we still have fires in our cellars, don't we?"

He pulled her closer and husked, "By God, Lilo, you still have the nicest body in our valley!"

She pushed at his hand. But it wouldn't budge. Kellermann's hands were strong. Her man was no longer young. But he still had the strength of a bull, and she whimpered with pleasure as he cut off her protestations with a firm but gentle kiss.

And then the door to their room burst open, and a voice shouted something they couldn't understand as a flashlight beam lashed in on them!

"Zum Teufel?" blinked Kellermann as he sat bolt upright in bed, shielding the woman with his body. Sergeant Compton repeated, "Stay right where you are and don't make a sound and you won't get hurt, folks!"

"Ich verstehe Sie nicht!" frowned Kellermann.

Compton said, "Just take it easy now," and snapped over his shoulder, "Hey, Krinke! Come in here and talk to these Krauts!"

Trooper Krinke, a husky young man from Lockport, New York, joined his sergeant in the doorway, grinned weirdly through his black-face, and said in stilted German, "Good evening, Mein Herr and gracious lady. The sergeant says you're to stay just as you are and nobody will be hurt. Do you understand?"

Kellermann asked, "Who are you? What are you doing here? We have nothing worth stealing. We are only poor farm folk!"

Krinke said, "We are American, uh (what the fuck was the German for paratrooper?) . . . American soldiers. We don't want to hurt you and we won't, if you do just as we say."

"Ask him not to shine that light in my face, young man. I am an old soldier. I know the form."

Krinke told Compton what he's been asked and added, "I'll light that lamp over there so we can see what's up around here."

Krinke went over to a bedside table and fumbled for a light switch. Kellermann said, "That's a kerosene lamp, you idiot. Tell that other idiot with the flashlight not to shoot me and I'll strike a match, damn it!"

Krinke laughed and said in English, "Feisty old fart,

ain't he?" Then he saw the frightened eyes of Frau Kellermann staring at him over the edge of the quilt and quickly added in German, "Don't worry, gracious lady. It's going to be all right. You have my word."

Kellermann struck a match. But his trembling hand betrayed him and it went out. He cursed and struck another as his wife asked Trooper Krink, "Are you a Negro?"

Kellermann muttered, "Hush, momma. It's burnt cork they have on their faces. We used to do the same at night on the western front." And this time he got the lamp to light. The sergeant in the doorway said something to the German-speaking trooper and Krinke said, "Don't either of you move for a moment. I have to search the room before we let you get up."

"I have a shotgun and a hunting rifle," said Kellermann. "They are in a case near the back door. I keep no guns in my bedroom. Do I look like a man who sleeps with a pistol under his pillow?"

Krinke ignored the remark as he swiftly searched the room, opening drawers and going through the one closet. He turned to Kellermann and said, "Stand up. Put your hands on top of your head." Then, as the surly farmer obeyed his order, Krinke patted him down on either side of his flannel nightgown. He turned and said, "They're clean, sarge."

Compton said, "Search the old broad."

Krinke replied, "Hey, for Christ's sake, sarge!"

"You heard me, trooper! A Kraut is a Kraut and I don't like surprises!"

Krinke ordered the middle-aged woman out of bed and said, "I'm sorry, gracious lady. I have to search you too."

"I have nothing, nothing!" the woman wailed, cowering away as she whimpered, "Don't touch me, you nigger! Horst! Don't let him touch me!"

Kellermann took a protective step toward his wife, and Compton snicked the bolt on his carbine, saying, "Freeze!"

A carbine round fell to the floor, and Kellermann knew the young American had made the useless gesture of reloading his weapon to get around the language barrier in a hurry. He stepped back and kept his hands very still as he husked, "Easy, momma. These men mean business!"

Frau Kellermann backed away from Trooper Krinke until her shoulder blades were against the wall. Then she screamed and said, "I have nothing under my nightgown, see?" as she raised the hem above her head, exposing her naked body to their full view. Krinke gasped and her husband shouted, "Stop that, you idiotic child!"

Frau Kellermann dropped her nightgown back in place and covered her face with her hands, sobbing, "Please don't touch me!"

Krinke turned to Compton and said, "I'd say she wasn't armed, wouldn't you, sarge?"

Compton grinned and replied, "Nice figure on the old girl too. Let's get them downstairs and see if the captain's there yet."

Krinke told the farmer and his wife what to do, and Kellermann picked up the kerosene lamp. He noticed, as they were leaving, that the American called Compton stooped to pick up the live round he'd spilled on the floor as a warning. These young men were professionals. Every move they made was calculated. That made things simpler. If he and momma cooperated, they'd be all right. Green troops were the ones you had to worry about. Men who knew the trade seldom committed atrocities.

As they were going down the stairs, he whispered to his wife, "We must do everything they say, momma. No more foolishness, eh?"

"They are going to rape me! I just know these niggers are going to rape me!"

"Hush, momma. Nobody's going to rape you. I won't let them. You'll see, everything will be all right!"

"You won't give me to them, will you, Horst?"

"Of course not. They'll have to kill me first. But be nice to them. They are as frightened as we are. I am an old soldier and I know about such things!"

Trooper Krinke, overhearing them on the stairs, made a mental note to warn the other guys about the crazy old broad. She had a nice shape for such an old bag, and she'd yell her head off if anybody got fresh with her. The old guy reminded him of his Uncle Franz. The one with the famous temper. You could push Uncle Franz just so far, and then he sort of came unglued and started taking things apart. The old Kraut looked strong too. He had to be over fifty, but he was all muscle under that dopey nightgown. Yeah, the guys would have to treat his old lady with respect.

Downstairs, the kitchen was crowded with paratroopers and a pair of grinning Russian farmworkers. One of the Russians went over to Kellermann and jeered, "They have you now, Nazi pig!"

Then he spit in Kellermann's face.

Captain Evans snapped, "That's enough of that!" and one of the troopers pulled the Russian away from the farmer. Kellermann stared soberly at the Russian and said, "You had a year to do that before your friends arrived, Boris. How come you waited so long?"

"They killed your dog!" sneered the Russian. "They clubbed his head flat with a rifle butt and slashed his throat! These men know how to deal with Nazi dogs!"

Kellermann shrugged, went to the sink, and sponged his face off with a dish towel as Evans asked Compton, "Anybody else in the house, sergeant?"

"Just these two and the Russians we picked up out back, captain. Those G2 reports were right on the money."

"You searched every room?"

"Sure we did, captain. There's an empty room up there with a pair of twin beds. But nobody's been using them lately. Had some pictures of Kraut GIs on the wall. Looks like they got a couple of kids working for Adolf."

Evans nodded and turned to Krinke, saying, "You stay with them, Krinke. These Russians speak German. So we'll keep the four of them together. But tell the Russians to behave themselves. Where's Corporal Muller?"

Trooper Murphy said, "With Mister Price, captain. The Limey's missing a parapack and Muller went with him to look for it."

"Go and get them, Murph. Sergeant Compton?"

"Sir?"

"I'm putting you in charge of the house. I don't want anyone moving around outside. Have one of your men dig a slit latrine in the basement. Better dig a private one in a corner for the woman. But make sure the cellar doors are bolted from the outside before you leave her down there alone. I want all exits secured before the sun comes up. You got that?"

"Yessir. But why can't this Kraut dig the latrine? He looks strong enough to put to work."

"Negative. I don't want that big mother's hands on a pick, a shovel, or anything else he can swing. We keep all four civilians right here in the kitchen where they can't get cute."

Kellermann said something in German, and Trooper Krinke explained, "He wants to know can he and his wife get dressed, captain."

Evans said, "Negative. Tell him they can put their coats on, if they're cold. But no pants and no shoes. If either of them make a break for it, it's a barefooted seven miles to the nearest telephone!"

Krinke explained this to the farmer who launched into another complaint about his uninvited guests. Krinke frowned and told Evans, "He says his cows have to be milked in less than an hour. He says the cows get sick if you don't milk them regular."

Evans glanced at his watch and said, "Let one of the Russians do it. We're going to have to take a chance, come daybreak, on these Ivans. Do you think I can trust this Kraut to tell me the truth about something, Krinke?"

"I don't know, sir. He says he's an old soldier and willing to be reasonable. But a Nazi is a Nazi, after all."

Kellermann understood just enough to protest, "Ich bin kein Nazi! Nur ein Bauer bin ich!"

Krinke smiled thinly and said, "He says he's not a Nazi. I'll bet he voted for Roosevelt in the last election too."

Evans said, "I want to know if these Russians were forced into working in Germany or whether they volunteered. According to G2, there's a difference."

One of the Russians understood just enough English to get the drift and said, in German, "Boris and I were captured near Leningrad. We had no choice in the matter."

Krinke ignored him to ask the farmer what he knew about it. Kellermann shrugged and said, "They were sent by the Todt Administration. They told me they were against Communism and wanted to work for the New Order. Until tonight, they acted very friendly and we were good to them. One never knows the bear that walks like a man until he chooses to show his fangs."

Krinke said, "The Kraut says they were volunteers, captain. But they seem to want to hand him his head right now."

Evans nodded and said, "I don't like guys with two faces. We'd better keep them inside. Get a couple of guys who know one end of a cow from the other and dig up some work clothes they can put on over their uniforms. We'll see to the livestock ourselves until we know everybody better. Do we have anybody who can sound like a Russian if he has to?"

Compton said, "Wolensky is a Polock from New Jersey, captain. He's out on the perimeter with Conti right now."

Evans nodded and said, "Get him into coveralls and tell him to make a lot of Slavic noise at anybody who noses around in the morning. Krinke, ask the Kraut if he's expecting visitors. A postman or somebody coming out from town to buy eggs, for instance."

Krinke spoke with the farmer, turned to the captain, and said, "No mail delivery for a couple of days, sir. But he says a forest ranger wanders in from the woods now and then for a glass of buttermilk and a chat."

"You'd better be the other guy in work clothes, Krinke. Anyone comes to call, get him off the road some way and take care of him the best way you can."

"Yessir. You want them captured or killed?"

"Whichever way is easier. You guys here at the farm are going to have to play it by ear until Price and I get back from our first recon. I don't want to leave too many bodies stinking up the joint. But if anyone gives you a hard time, use your knife. I don't want any noise either."

Murphy came back in with Price and Corporal Muller. Evans nodded at them and said, "We're going for a walk, Mister Price. Muller, I'll need you in case we have to discuss the weather with any Krauts. How good is your German?"

Muller said, "I can maybe find my way to the shithouse in German, captain. But I'm not too fluent."

"Can you say stick 'em up?"

"Yessir. That's Hände hoch!"

"That's good enough. I can't think of anything else I want to say to any Kraut at the moment. Murphy, I'm taking you too. The four of us have fourteen miles to travel before the sun comes up."

Price said, "It'll be dawn in less than three hours, Evans. You lot may be able to run fourteen miles in that time. But I can't. I'm not in shape!"

Evans said, "You'll be surprised what a man can do when he has to, Price. Let's go. We could have covered a quarter of a mile in the time we've been bullshitting about it!"

○○○

The German ambulance drove slowly in the dark as its driver watched the side of the road in the dim blue glow of his blackout beams. On a litter in back of him, Joseph Yellowpony moaned and tried to move, but he was strapped to the litter. A German medic put a hand on his shoulder and said, "Easy, comrade. You have a compound fracture and you must not move."

The words were in German, and they penetrated through to the semiconscious Yellowpony as a confused babble. He knew it wasn't English and so he replied in Dakota. The German medic had never heard Dakota before and thought the singsong sound was a cry of pain. He said, "They will give you morphine when we get you to the hospital, comrade. I know it hurts. But you must lay very still!"

Yellowpony looked around at the blurred faces in the Spirit Lodge and said, "I am Yellowpony and I count coup! I have just jumped out of a thunderbird with a broken wing and my medicine is good!"

A shadow said, "You must wake up, Two Persons. Your enemies have captured you and this is no time for counting coup."

Yellowpony protested, "You mustn't call me by my medicine name, grandfather! Joseph Yellowpony is the name I give the real world to call me by."

"We know you, inside yourself, as Two Persons, son of Man Who Walks Alone. We taught you your medicine name out alone beneath the August stars, remember?"

"I remember, grandfather. The stars were falling that night and I thought perhaps I might choose Falling Star as my medicine name. But I thought of who I was, and how it was with our people, and I knew who I was. I knew I was Two Persons, called by my brothers Yellowpony, and by the white-eyes, Joseph."

The ghost said, "By any name you are a Dakota. One of the Real People. That is what you must remember now. No more of this nonsense about counting coup. Let the white-eyes give you medals for your victories. They laugh at our feathers anyway!"

"You laughed at me, grandfather. You said we were red white-men when we tried to form our warrior society at Pine Ridge that time. Five times I jumped out of an airplane, and you laughed when I came home on leave with my silver wings. You said no man of my generation could join any of the old medicine lodges. Why did you laugh at us, grandfather. *We* are warriors too!"

The ghost said, "You are soldiers of the Long Knife. There is no such medicine society as that. You and the other men spoke of foolish things. We never had pool tables or Coca Cola machines in the Medicine Lodge of the Dog Soldiers!"

The ambulance hit a bump and a shaft of pain lanced through Yellowpony's broken leg. He moaned aloud, and it seemed his grandfather said, "Be careful! Remember you are a Dakota!"

Yellowpony lapsed into English to complain, "Some Dakota! I'm just another fucking blanket Injun off the reservation. I'm not a Dog Soldier or a Crooked Lance. I'm not even a fucking Contrary!"

The ghost insisted on speaking Dakota as it said, "The Dog Soldiers are all dead. The Crooked Lance is no more. They have taken away our Ghost Shirts and made us into Almost Men. Do you really think you could survive a Sundance, Two Persons?"

"I could if I had to," sighed Yellowpony, picturing himself and Jerry Bluefeather hanging from a lodge-pole with skewers through their flesh. He chuckled in his morphine haze and said, "Jerry Bluefeather might chicken out. But I'm as tough as you ever were, grandfather. You may have had the scars on your chest. But I never saw you turn down any government rations either!"

"Remember that when the Germans question you, Two Persons! Remember they are only white-eyes, and that *you* are a *Dakota!*"

"Fuck 'em all but six," said Joseph Yellowpony, as the ambulance hit another bump. The pain was terrible. But he grinned wolfishly and insisted, "I can take it. I can take anything the fucking Krauts can dish out!"

ooo

Matt Price had been right. He couldn't run worth a damn. But nothing was moving in the gray morning fog as the four of them crouched on a wooded rise overlooking Fabrik Vogelbach.

Price looked up at the sky and muttered, "It's gettin perishing bright! How do we get back through those bloody woods in broad bloody daylight?"

Evans said, "I'll worry about that. What do you think about that installation? Is it anything like the one you worked on in Spain?"

Price nodded down at the bewildering mass of brick buildings and towering steel columns and said, "It seems to be laid out much the same. You see those things that look like aircraft hangars made out of brick? Those are the retorts. The thing that looks like a locomotive standing on its head is the catalytic chamber. Those ten-story silos on the other side are the cracking towers. The tank farm is out of sight on the other side, by the railway siding and the docks."

Evans grimaced and said, "The whole mess looks like somebody crossed a steel mill with a big brick church and let the offspring dress itself in an erector set. That canal over there must be the one leading to the Rhine, eh?"

"Yes. They've canalized the original brook with locks. If all else fails, we could damage the locks and leave a lot of barges stranded in the mud."

"Shit, they'd fix that in a couple of days. We've got to put that plant permanently out of the war!"

"Nothing's permanent, Yank. By the way, isn't Evans a Welsh name?"

"I guess it was, a long time ago. But let's not worry about my fucking family tree, Price. How many men do you think we have to take out to get you in there?"

"I don't know. There can't be all that many workers in there. The hydrogenation is a batch process. You need a few hands to lay the coal beds and get them to burning right. Once you have the coal incandescent, you feed in steam and oxygen until the bed's used up. Then you shut it down and start all over again."

"I know that. Our best bet would be to slip in while the gas is brewing off. How often do you think they rebuild the coal beds?"

"Hard to say. A few inches more or less of coal could mean a full day of production. We were working on a continuous feed idea at Toledo. But the coal beds are not the bottle neck. The catalytic chamber is. You can only push so much hot gas in at a time. I see they have storage tanks between the cat chambers and the cracking towers too. Looks like they let the liquid hydrocarbon build up between runs. The cracking towers run 'round the clock."

Trooper Murphy hissed, "Truck convoy coming down the pike, sir!"

"I see them," Evans said. "The concentration camp's up that way. Must be bringing workers to the plant."

He took a pair of binoculars from his harness and propped his elbows in the fir needles to steady them as he zeroed in on the plant gate. Price said, "There's your answer, Yank! It's hot and dirty work to lay a new coal bed. The perishing Jerries are letting prisoners do the narsty."

Evans said, "Shut up. I'm trying to see how tight the security is down there. Corporal Muller?"

"Yessir?"

"The guards on the truck are wearing navy blue or black. Does that spell SS to you?"

"Could be, sir. But the Kraut Panzer uniform is black, and the Waffen SS wears the same shade of olive gray as the regular army."

"The two guys on the gate look like US post office types. Blue gray is Luftwaffe, isn't it?"

"Yessir. Air force, anti-aircraft gunners, and paratroopers. The Panzer Grenadiers wear gray too. I don't know who the fuck *they* belong to!"

"Herman Goering," grunted Evans. "The fat boy heads up the Luftwaffe and has his own private army besides. Those gate guards must be air defense jerks. That squares with the fuel they're making down there being slated for the Luftwaffe."

Through the field glasses, Evans saw one of the guards slide the chain link gate to one side for the trucks. He waved them through and Evans muttered, "No trip ticket. You just have to show up with a truckload of workers. If the fence is electrified, I didn't see either of them throw a switch before they touched the gate!"

Muller asked, "Can you make out their weapons, sir? They look like rifles from here."

"They are. Bolt-action carbines. Panzer Grenadiers and paratroops carry submachine guns, don't they?"

"Yessir. Schmeiser nine millimeters. Their infantry carries one to a squad."

"Which means these are rear-echelon guys with second-string weapons. The goddamn guards on the trucks didn't seem to have *any* guns. What the fuck keeps those prisoners from taking off like big-ass birds?"

Price said, "I can answer that. It's called *fear*. Saw a lot of that in Spain one time. The prisoners don't run because they have no place to run to. They must have rounded that lot up in Eastern Europe, and they wouldn't know how to get home in those perishing striped pajamas if they *did* get away."

Evans nodded and said, "They must be trusties. G2 said the camp here was easier on the nerves than most." He lowered the field glasses thoughtfully and mused, "Now, if we could just get past those two lousy guards . . ."

Murphy asked, "Why don't we just sneak up on them as soon as it's dark again, captain? It's a good 200 yards of nothing in both directions. We could knock 'em off, open the gate, and . . ."

"Negative. I want to get Mister Price, here, inside without the Nazis knowing he's been there. Let's circle around and see what they've got going for them on the canal side. According to our photos, the railroad spur and barge docks don't look very secure."

Price grabbed his shoulder and husked, "You must be mad! It's broad bloody *daylight*, Yank!"

Evans shrugged his hand away and said, "Look, I tried to get them to stop the sun for us. But my name wasn't Joshua and the people upstairs don't seem to care what I want down here. Let's move it on out. Muller, you take the point. Murphy brings up the rear and acts as getaway man if we blow it. You stay with me, Mister Price."

"You're mad. I'm not budging from here until it gets dark again, damn it!"

Evans got to his feet and said, "Yes you are. Murphy

will kill you if you get more than ten yards from me. You got that, Murph?"

"Yessir. You'd better stick close to the captain, Mister Price."

ooo

A telephone rang in Berlin and a sleep-drugged hand reached out in the wan gray light of morning. The man in the bed put the receiver to his ear and muttered, "Here speaks Oberst Von Dreihausen, OKW."

The voice at the other end of the line was excited as it said, "Here speaks Steiner from the Paris office. Something very funny was going on last night. A British Mosquito flew into a barrage-balloon cable near Lyons."

Von Dreihausen swore and muttered, "You wake me up at this hour to tell me we nailed a British bomber?"

"There's more to it than that, Herr Oberst! One of the men in the plane lived through it! The bomber lost a wing, spun in, and exploded. But this one survivor somehow managed to parachute to the ground. He broke his leg in the landing and . . ."

"Listen, damn it! I've been up all night and my eyes are killing me! Question the damned Englishman and don't call me back unless his name is Winston Churchill!"

"Herr Oberst, the survivor was not an Englishman. He

82

was an American paratrooper!"

The man in Berlin sat up in bed and mused, "So? Lyons is a little deep inside France to find an American paratrooper. Where is he now?"

"They're holding him at a Luftwaffe hospital near Lyons, Herr Oberst."

"You'd better get over there and see what he has to say, then. Make sure the damned Gestapo doesn't get to him in the meantime. Those Jew-beating idiots don't know the first thing about interrogating a prisoner. What do we have on him so far?"

"His name is Joseph Yellowpony, and he seems to be a Red Indian. They saved his leg and he's out of danger. But he keeps saying dreadful things to the nurses. The swine has no apparent gratitude for all the trouble it was to keep him alive last night!"

"I have something else about paratroopers in Mosquitos that seems to tie in with this madness. Catch a Storch to Lyons and see what you can get out of him. You know how to make a prisoner talk, don't you?"

Von Dreihausen hung up and lay back on the pillow, willing his mind to let go, sweet Jesus, long enough to get an hour's sleep.

After a time he rubbed his tired eyes and sat up, muttering, "It's no use. I'll never sleep now, until I find out what the devil this is all about!"

○○

Dave Evans hissed, "Down!" as he saw Corporal Muller give the hand signal for "Enemy sighted!"

He pushed Price into a clump of bushes, pumped his arm three times for Murphy, to his rear, to see. Then he joined Price in the bushes and waited what seemed a million years.

Somewhere in the forest, a linnet sang about spring. There were no other sounds for a time. Then Evans heard a metallic click and said, "That's Muller's toy cricket. It's the all clear signal."

Evans got back to his feet and moved silently toward the sound he'd heard. Price followed, doing his best to walk silently in the dry forest duff.

They came to where Corporal Muller stood over an olive green form on the forest floor. Muller pointed at the body with the knife in his hand and said, "Never knew what hit him. He was walking through the woods like a big-ass bird."

Evans stared down at the dead German. He'd been a

middle-aged man with a slight paunch. His eyes stared dully up at the sky between the treetops, and there was a faint sneer on his lips. Evans noted the gold eagle on the olive green tunic and said, "Forestry service. Why didn't you let him pass on by?"

Muller said, "I tried to. But he spotted me and asked who I was. I answered in German and told him I was a charcoal burner. He put a hand on that bitty whore pistol on his belt and asked to see my papers. I showed the nosey bastard my papers. I think I hit him in the aorta with the first thrust. He dropped like a sack of shit, you know?"

Evans swept his eyes over the three stab wounds just above the dead German's belt and said, "We'd better bury him. Look for a fallen log, Muller. The earth will be soft under fallen timber, and we want him at least three feet under."

"We didn't bring no entrenching tools," protested corporal Muller.

Evans shrugged and said, "Use your knife and hands, then. We can't let anyone find him for a few days, and he's sure to be missed sooner or later."

Trooper Murphy came up to them, stared down at the dead man, and whistled softly. Evans said, "Don't bunch up like this. Get down the slope a few yards and keep an eye on the road, Murph."

Murphy nodded and moved away through the fir needles. Evans turned to Price and said, "You'd better help Muller get rid of this body, Mister Price."

Price nodded and muttered, "Least we can do for the sod, I suppose. But, tell me, captain; who's going to bury *me*, when you get us killed?"

○○○

The OKW man wore a Wehrmacht officer's uniform and
a friendly smile as he sat down by Yellowpony's hospital
bed. The Amerind was in traction. His leg cast hung in a
pulley sling over the bed, and the bed had been cranked
up, leaving Yellowpony in a semireclining position. The
OKW man spoke English as he offered Yellowpony a
cigarette and said, "I am Major Steiner. I trust you have
been treated well, my friend?"

Yellowpony accepted the cigarette, waited until the
German gave him a light, and said, "Fuck you, Major
Steiner. You're not my friend. You're my enemy. All you
get is name, rank, and serial number."

"Very well, let us start with your rank then. Your
identity tags give your name as one Joseph Yellowpony.
But there were no rank badges on that camouflaged uniform you had on when they found you."

"No shit? I guess you'll have to guess my rank, then.
I don't give nothing away for free, Kraut."

Steiner sighed and said, "You seem to have seen too

86

many of those Hollywood movies about us, ah, Joseph. I can promise you your full rights under the rules of the Geneva Convention. You have nothing to gain by this rudeness. You are setting up a straw man just in order to knock it down. What harm can there be in according one another common courtesy? We are both soldiers, albeit on opposite sides at the moment. We have nothing to gain by trading foolish insults."

Yellowpony shrugged and said, "Okay. I want a T-bone steak, smothered in mushrooms. Then ask that pretty little blond nurse if she wants to fuck. I think her name is Ursula."

"You will be fed the same rations as our troops. I doubt if you'll be up to sex for some time. Would you like me to see if I can get you some brandy?"

"Shit yes. I'm a regular drunken Injun. Everybody knows we spill our guts with a little firewater inside us. Didn't you know that, Kraut?"

"I assumed you might be an American Indian. What, ah, tribe do you belong to?"

"The Lonesome Polecat Tribe. Our reservation is just a mile outside of Dogpatch!"

"Dogpatch? What State is that in, please?"

"West Virginia, I think. It might be in Kentucky. I ain't been home since Sadie Hawkins Day."

Steiner nodded and said, "Tell me, what did you do before you were drafted into the American army?"

Yellowpony was about to protest that he'd volunteered for the troops. But he caught himself and said soberly, "I had a heap good job before the war. I used to stand outside a cigar store, holding up three wooden cigars."

Steiner frowned and said, "I think you are trying to pull my leg, Joseph Yellowpony!"

"All right. I'll tell you what I really did in civilian life."

He took a deep drag, blew the smoke in the German's face, and said, "I used to carve obscene totem poles for the tourist trade. My best-selling model was a big growly bear with an eight-inch dick!"

Steiner frowned and said, "You are being very stupid. We know all about the mission you were on last night."

"No shit? Then why are you asking me about it? I'm not about to give you the right time, Kraut!"

"You will tell us everything. We do not wish to cause you any discomfort. But if you force our hand, we can be most unpleasant. Do you understand what I am saying, Joseph Yellowpony?"

Yellowpony took the cigarette from his mouth, casually raised his other hand, and slowly snuffed the glowing tobacco out on the back of his left wrist.

The German sat, frozen faced, as the smell of burnt human flesh filled the room. Then Yellowpony smiled at him pleasantly and said, "Your move, Kraut."

○○

Sergeant Conti lay on his belly in a clump of what he sincerely hoped was not poison ivy, watching the dirt road winding up to the farm through the fir trees. It was starting to warm up, and the shoe polish he'd stained his jump suit with smelled funny, mixed with sweat. The burnt cork on his face itched. It felt like he'd walked through a spider web. It felt like that night in Fairmont Park when he and Linda had walked under the trees and through the orb of a garden spider that had spun its web right across the path. Boy, had Linda ever screamed. You'd have thought it was *his* idea to walk into that web, for Christ's sake!

Conti heard a soft cricket chirp and turned to see a man from Compton's stick crawling toward him through the brush. What was the guy's name? Oh, yeah, Gilmore. He was some kind of hillbilly from Arkansas or someplace like that.

Gilmore reached Conti's position and handed over a warm, closed mess kit, saying, "I brung you some chow from the house, sarge. The old German lady's a tolerable cook, and Compton thought you might be getting hungry."

Conti thanked Gilmore and opened the mess kit. He sniffed suspiciously and asked, "What the fuck *is* it?"

"Red cabbage and pork biled in apple sauce or some sech shit, sarge. The funny white things is potato dumplings. Try some of it. It's right toler'ble chow, considering."

Conti unhooked a spoon from the mess kit handle and tasted cautiously. Then he nodded and said, "You're right. It's not too bad at that. How are they maknig out back at the house?"

"We're getting on. The old woman's keepin' busy in the kitchen and we've mostly been eating. The old man got out some likker. They calls it snaps or something. But old Compton won't let us drink none. He had Krinke tell the old man to put it away. Compton sure acts chickenshit sometimes."

Conti chewed another mouthful, swallowed, and said, "It's getting late. The captain should have gotten back by now."

"You think the Krauts got him and them other old boys?"

"I don't know."

"Well, why don't we send us out a patrol to look for 'em?"

"Because we can't. The worse thing we could do would be to spread the outfit all over hell until nobody knew where anybody was. If the others are still out there, they may be pinned down someplace, waiting for a chance to work their way back. We go pussy-footing after them, and we're liable to run into whatever it is that's keeping them from coming back!"

"Yeah, but what if the damn Germans has *catched* 'em, sarge? What if they been catched and start tellin' them old German boys where *we* is?"

Conti chewed another mouthful and said, "We'll be up

shit creek without a paddle. Is this your first jump, Gilmore?"

"Well, sort of."

"It's my third. But I remember how it was the first time. I made my first jump under The War Lord, in Sicily. Man, I didn't know *what* the fuck was going on until he got us back to our own lines. I used to ask a lot of what-ifs, buddy. Nobody ever gave me any answers I could understand, and after a while, I stopped asking. Now I just take a look at what's coming down the pike and either salute, shoot, drink, eat, smoke, or fuck it. If I run into something that I can't figure out, I get a detail together and paint it white. The thing is, I don't waste time *thinking*. Thinking is not part of a soldier's job."

Gilmore nodded soberly and said, "A man could get nervous in the service, did he think too much about ever'thing that could happen in a war. But you're the senior noncom, sarge."

"So?"

"Well, some of the fellers was talkin' about it, back to the house. They was wondering did you have a plan, did the captain get his fool self shot or something."

Conti shrugged and said, "We don't know he's been shot. He could be coming back anytime now."

"Yeah. But what if he ain't? Sergeant Compton says nobody never told him shit about how we'uns is supposed to git our ownselves *outten* here when the time comes."

Conti stared down at the empty road in front of his position and said, "Compton worries too much. You'd better get back to the house and hold his hand, Gilmore."

"What are we a-gonna *do,* sarge?" Gilmore insisted.

Conti said, "You'll do as you're *told,* soldier! Get back to the house and keep out of sight. Do you want me to put it in writing?"

Gilmore muttered, "Shoot! This is purely one chickenshit old outfit!" as he crawled away. Conti took another bite of food and wondered why he didn't feel very hungry now.

He scratched at the soot on his neck and tried not to think about the captain not coming back. He'd asked the captain about their evacuation plans. But the captain had said it was classified.

Maybe some planes were coming in to pick them up after they'd completed the mission. That was probably it. They had the R-300 pack, and the captain would radio for a lift home when they were through here. How far were they from England and what was the range of an R-300 anyway? He remembered calling for air support in Sicily on an R-300. But that Navy carrier had only been ten or twenty miles away and there'd been a hell of a lot of static.

Maybe the one they had now was a new model. Maybe they *could* reach clear to England with the one the captain had. He wouldn't have brought it if he couldn't *talk* to anyone on it, and there was nobody around *here* but the fucking *Krauts!*

Conti looked at his watch and got to his hands and knees. He crawled a few yards through the brush, and then he had the ridge between himself and the road and could move in a crouching walk. He moved along the perimeter, clicking his toy cricket from time to time. After a while he heard an answering click and nodded approvingly. Trooper Blanchard, up ahead, was playing invisible man. He found Blanchard behind a fallen fir tree, buried under a pile of loose branches, and said, "I'll get one of Compton's guys to relieve you in an hour. How's it going on this side?"

Blanchard said, "Man, I had a bead on a deer just now you wouldn't believe! The motherfucker's antlers were something else! I'll bet I never get a shot at a trophy like that if I hunt a million years! It took off just before you got here. Must have heard you coming."

"That's good," said Conti. "Deer browsing in the woods means the woods are empty. You listen to the birds too. When the song birds stop and you start hearing crows, it means something's moving out there in the trees."

Blanchard snorted, "Shit, I know that, sarge. I was one hunting son of a bitch back home in Iowa. Used to go hunting with my dad every fall. But we never got us a deer like that motherfucker I just saw. They say there's wild pigs in these woods too."

"Could be," Conti said. "We're just south of the Black Forest Game Preserve."

Blanchard asked, "What do I do if one of them wild pigs comes at me? I hear they're liable to go for a man with their tusks!"

"You just worry about Krauts. I don't think any wild animal will charge you if you leave it alone."

"Yeah. But what if one does? I'll have to *shoot* it, won't I?"

"You shoot that carbine without one damned good reason and you can save your soul for Jesus, because your ass will belong to *me!*"

"Damn it, sarge, a wild boar snuffin' through the brush at me might be a damned good reason! What the hell am I supposed to do if one of them things comes at me?"

"Make friends with it. I've got to see how Lewis is making out."

Conti moved on, muttering, "Wild pigs, for Christ's sake!" under his breath. Blanchard was getting edgy. All this waiting, with nothing to do, was getting on all their nerves. When he and Sergeant Compton changed places he'd have to think up some shit detail to keep his guys busy. It was funny how he'd never understood that when he was a private. But you had to keep GIs busy and bitching, or they started to worry about the damndest things.

He smiled to himself. *Jesus, you're getting to be a GI*

noncom, Junior! Like those chickenshit old sergeants back at Benning! I'll bet some of the guys think you've had stripes up since the Spanish-American War. But you really don't know what the fuck you're doing, do you?

He wondered if Sergeant Marvin had felt like this when they'd jumped in Sicily that first time. Jesus, he'd thought Sergeant Marvin had invented the war in those days. But Marvin couldn't be that much older than he was. Had the old War Lord been as confused and worried inside as he was right now? He'd never gotten to know Marvin very well before they transferred him out. The guy had looked and acted like he ate bullets for breakfast. But now that Conti was wearing stripes, he wasn't so sure. How the fuck had a Guinea from South Philly got himself into this?

His folks had raised him to be a *barber*. He *knew* something about *cutting hair,* for God's sake! But what the fuck was he supposed to do if the captain didn't come back and he found himself in command of this mission?

○○○

"This is a hell of a way to run a railroad!" said Dave
Evans as he focused the field glasses on the coaling facili-
ties across the narrow canal. He and the others had
managed to work their way along a finger of hedged-in
fields and orchards between Fabrik Vogelbach and the
hospital complex. Evans peered through a hedge with an
apple orchard to his rear; a service road and the canal
ran to his right and left beyond an open strip of field less
than 300 yards in width. From this angle, the approaches
to the hydrogenation plant were guarded only by the
width of the canal and two lines of chain-link fencing.
One fence ran between the service road and the canal,
apparently just to keep kids and stray dogs from falling
in. It was only twelve feet high, and any schoolboy could
be over it in a flash. The fence on the plant side of the
canal had a roll of concertina barbed wire running along
the top. But concertina was no sweat for a trained soldier
to get through. The bottom edge of the chain-link mesh
was embedded in cement, meaning nobody could burrow

under it in a hurry—but also meaning it was grounded. The fence couldn't be electrified.

Things were looking up.

Evans turned to Price, crouched at his side, and said, "The photo-montage showed three fence lines. But they were blurred. The edges of the concrete apron under the fence gave us three lines on the photos. Shadows and our own paranoia did the rest. I can't believe the security's so lax, even this far behind the German lines! They must be saving their barbed wire for the Channel defenses!"

"Don't be cocky, Yank," warned Price. "The Fascists believe in defense in depth. Jerry always spreads his front line thin, then backs it up with one thin ruddy line after another. They'll have security checkpoints between the different parts of the plant. You see them ruddy lamp poles all about inside? Once the sun goes down, they'll have the whole place lit like Times Square in New York!"

Evans nodded and said, "That's why there's no point in waiting for it to get dark." He swept the field glasses down the canal and mused, "There are three barges tied up down there by that coal tipple. Nobody moving down there either. We could cross the canal by jumping across from one barge to the other. Then, if we shinnied up inside the coal tipple, there's a conveyor belt running deep inside the plant. I can't see where it goes after it ducks between those cracking towers. But it must run pretty close to the reducing ovens, don't you think?"

"Garn! We'd never make it that way! We'd be like ruddy ducks in a shooting gallery, running along that overhead conveyor against the flaming sky!"

"Never run when you can walk," said Evans. "A running man draws attention from a mile away. Few people notice a *walking* figure at any distance."

"They'd bloody well notice one walking above them in yon sky, mate! I still say we should scrag the gate guards, blast our way in, and do as much damage as we can in fifteen minutes. I calculate something like twenty-five between the time they hear the shots at the concentration camp, decide to look into it, and move in cautious. By then, we could have it done and be off."

"You could really screw that cat chamber up in, say, eight or ten minutes?"

"I bloody can—I can have it shut down in three."

"Yeah. But you're talking about destroying it. I liked your thoughts on screwing it up so they don't know about it better! How long would that take, Price?"

"An hour or more. I'd have to cover my tracks a bit after I sabotaged the ruddy valves. Be a perishing waste of time if Jerry knew they'd been tinkered with. The whole idea is to let Jerry run the process at the wrong settings until he gums things up for fair, see? I mean, the idea was to make him shut down for repairs a dozen times before he figured out what was *wrong* with the bloody machinery!"

"All right. We have to figure some way to give you at least an hour to fuck around in there."

"Coo! What's Jerry going to be doing all this time, looking over my ruddy shoulder and offering helpful suggestions?"

Corporal Muller had been listening to the exchange and he said, "I got an idea, sir. Krinke and me both speak German. Why don't we knock out the gate guards and change places with them? If we waited until just after they changed guards, before moving in, we'd have at least two hours before the next shift and . . ."

Evans cut in to say, "Negative. For two reasons. Number one, the corporal of the guard would be coming by to check more than once a tour of duty. If you nailed him before he noticed you were not the men he'd posted at the gate, the *sergeant* of the guard would miss *him* in less than half an hour. Knock off the sergeant and the officer of the day is going to come looking for *him*. We'd wind up with the last act of Hamlet around that gate. This might not be so bad. But that takes us to reason number two. We don't want the Krauts to know we've been inside. They may not be too bright. But I sort of think they'd start to wonder why we wiped out a whole guard mount, and once they started looking around inside, they'd dope it out for themselves!"

Price ran a thumbnail through the stubble on his jaw and mused, "I think the lad's on the right track, Evans. There's a way 'round it, you know. What if I were to plant some charges somewhere else in the plant? Say, under the cracking towers?"

"We can't do that. The explosion would flatten everything for half a mile in every direction!" He gestured over his shoulder with a thumb and added, "The hospital's only a quarter mile or so from here. Just behind those trees back there!"

Price nodded and insisted, "I know that. But Jerry can't know we've orders to be so flaming gentle! I wasn't talking about blowing up the cracking towers. I was talking about placing some charges to do it, and then forgetting to light the ruddy fuse!"

Evans frowned and asked, "Isn't that a little obvious?"

Price said, "Not if I did it right. I could doctor the fuses to be defective, see? I'd light the master fuse above a sort of accidental crimp that sort of accidentally spilled a few inches of fuse powder in the confusion. Jerry would think we'd done a poor job of work. Then he'd thank his stars we hadn't done it right."

"It might work." Evans said. "How long would it be before they noticed their catalytic process wasn't working right?"

"How long do you want it to take? I can fix it to run more or less proper for a day or so."

"No more than that? It's timing it pretty close."

"If I muck about with the valves, things are sure to start falling apart in, say, eighteen hours or so. The Jerry technicians will adjust the valves and get things running right for a bit. I don't know how long they'll tinker with the valves before they see they just have to shut her down for repairs. But it should keep them hopping for some time before they figure what I've done!"

Evans shook his head and said, "It just won't work if they know we've been in there."

He looked at his wrist and said, "Let's get back to the Kellermann farm. I've got to think some more about this."

Price asked, "Are we going back *now?* It's seven perishing miles in broad bloody *daylight,* Yank!"

"We can't sit *here* all day! Muller, I want you to take the point again. What do you think our best route figures to be?"

Muller said, "Through the Indian country between the roads, captain. The Krauts are starting to move a lot of stuff on the road net now."

"You think you know the way back, sticking to the tall timber and avoiding every road and trail?"

"I hope so, sir."

"Don't hope, Muller. You'd better be *sure!*"

Muller shrugged and said, "You'd better take the point then, captain. I'm only sure of the general direction."

Evans shook his head and said, "Do the best you can, corporal. I'm not sure I know *that* for certain!"

○○

Two Persons swung around the Sundance pole and waited for the voice of Wakan Tonka to speak to him. It was said that some braves prayed as they swung around the Sundance pole. But grandfather said it was better medicine if one waited for the Great Spirit to notice you in His own good time. The pain was worse than Two Persons had imagined it would be. But he knew he would not cry out. He had cried when he was a child. But not since he'd become a man at the age of nine. He'd counted coup at nine. Those white-eyes at the Boy Scout camp had caught him stealing a bag of flour and taken turns whipping him with their belts. But he had not cried, and later, he'd crept back in the night and taken a whole carton of food and the troop leader's pants. Grandfather had laughed to hear of it. But when he'd asked grandfather for a feather, the old man had knocked him down and started drinking again. Grandfather sometimes drank too much and his eyes bothered him when you asked him about the old ways.

Two Persons wondered if grandfather was watching from the Other Place and why this Sundance was being done so strangely. Why was he hanging from a skewer through his leg, upside down, instead of the usual way? It was hard to keep one's thoughts together, swinging around the pole head-down like this. . . .

A voice came down from the pinwheeling stars to ask, "What is your name!"

Two Persons was surprised to hear Wakan Tonka speak to him in English. He muttered, *"You* know me as Two Persons. Real people call me Yellowpony."

The German officer grinned at the doctor across the bed and murmured, "Now we're getting somewhere! He says he has two identities. I *knew* he was OSS!"

The doctor nodded and said, "I told you scopolamine was the only way. The man has an incredible pain threshold!"

Two Persons swung among the stars, wondering why Wakan Tonka and that other spirit were speaking German now. He'd never heard that Wakan Tonka revealed himself to one in anything but Dakota. But maybe the spirits spoke in every language, like the white-eyed Jesus. It seemed logical, when one thought about it. Wakan Tonka had more medicine than any of the white-eyes' gods.

The voice called down to him, "How did you come to be where we found you, Yellowpony? What were you doing in that British plane?"

Two Persons said, "It wasn't fair. I had seniority on that fucking Italian. They only made Conti over me because I was a Dakota!"

Another OKW man at the foot of the bed whispered, "What was that about Italy, and what is a Dakota?"

"A Dakota is what the British call the American C-47 transport plane. It seems they might have been on their way to Italy. He keeps cursing some Italian called Conti.

Perhaps a member of the Italian partisan forces?"

"That makes no sense, Steiner. What were they doing over Lyons if they were working with the partisans behind our lines in the north of Italy?"

"It could have been a shuttle operation. You know, of course, about the American shuttle bombers who fly on to Russia for more fuel and bombs before returning from a run on Berlin?"

"The bastards hit Berlin flying both ways. Coming and going. But those Mosquitos were not on any bomb run!"

"They could have been carrying supplies and OSS advisors to the Italian Alps from England. Lyons is not too far off a great circle route to Italy and they were flying low. They may have swung a little north to avoid the French Central Massif."

The doctor warned, "You people will have to hurry, if you wish to question him further. I can't give him much more of the drug without killing him, in his condition."

Two Persons listened to the spirits speaking German among the stars and wondered what it was he was trying to remember. This was some kind of a test, he knew. But he couldn't remember what it was or how he'd gotten here to the ceremony. Grandfather had told him the Sundance wasn't held anymore. He'd said the white-eyes had forbidden the Sundance and the Ghostdance and burned all the Medicine Shirts after Wounded Knee. Grandfather and some of the other young men had tried to perform the Sundance after Wounded Knee. But the soldiers had cut them down from the pole and beaten them. Then the Indian Police had murdered Buffalo Bull Who Waits and the Real People had lost their medicine. . . .

"What were you taking to Italy, Joseph?" asked a faraway voice in English.

Two Persons answered in Dakota, asking, "Why do you call me Joseph, Wakan Tonka? That is not my *real* name. That is the name the Black Robes at the mission school gave me, remember?"

The voice said, "Speak English, Joseph. You must tell us in English why you were flying to Italy!"

Two Persons didn't answer until he'd swung around the pole a few times, considering the spirit words. His people taught only of one Great Spirit, Wakan Tonka, who was *good*. But the Cheyenne said there was another Great Spirit, called Wendigo, who was *evil*, like the Lucifer of the Black Robes. The Black Robes had told him of a bad thing some white-eyes did, with an upside-down cross and a lot of other things turned crazy and backward, like the old Contrary Lodge had behaved. The Contraries had ridden into battle backwards, striking out with the butt of their lances instead of the points. But the Contraries had been brave and good. Not like the devil worshippers the Black Robes talked about. He had to think about this very carefully. Why was this Sundance upside down in the dark? Why were the spirits talking to him in English and German? What sort of a test *was* this?

Steiner shook the injured paratrooper's shoulder and insisted, "What were you taking to the partisans, Joseps?"

Yellowpony answered, "Why can't you speak Dakota?" in his native tongue.

Steiner said, "I got something about a Dakota C-47. But the rest is gibberish. Who do we have that understands Red Indian?"

His companion said, "There's a Luftwaffe officer who's mother was an American with Indian blood. The Sioux tribe, as I recall. He might know a few words, if we could reach him. He's flying for Galland in sector Dora-Dora."

"We have no way of knowing this one's a Sioux," said Steiner. Then he bent over Yellowpony and asked, "Are you a Sioux, Joseph?"

Two Persons answered in Dakota, "Our enemies and

the white-eyes call us that. Some of our people are starting to use the word too. Calling a Dakota a Sioux is an insult. But a lot of our people have given up trying to correct the strangers. The sign at Pine Ridge says Sioux. The white-eyes have no feelings."

Steiner frowned and said in German, "I don't know what *that* was all about. But I seem to have insulted him. Apparently he is from some other tribe."

The other OKW man said, "That singsong gibberish could be anything. It could take us a week to find someone who could figure out what dialect he's using. I understand there are something like 500 Red Indian languages. It would be easier to teach him German!"

"I'll get it out of the swine in English!" Steiner growled, shaking Yellowpony again and saying, "You must speak English, Joseph. We are your friends. You must speak to us so that we understand you."

In blurred English, Yellowpony muttered, "Fuck you, Wendigo!"

"What means this Wendigo?" whispered the man at the foot of the bed. Steiner raised a warning hand and bent low over Yellowpony to ask insistently, "Was Wendigo one of the men with you, Joseph?"

Two Persons swung across the sky, laughing softly among the pinwheeling stars, and asked in English, "What's the matter with you ghosts? Don't you even know your own commanding officer?"

Steiner swore and said, "We gave him too much of the drug. *Now* he's speaking nonsense in *English!*"

The other OKW man paled and said, "Not so fast! I think Wendigo is a code name for Der Fuhrer! He just said Wendigo was *our* commanding officer!"

Steiner gasped, "They wouldn't dare!" Then he shook the semiconscious man and asked, "Why do you use a code name for Hitler?"

Yellowpony grinned and recited, "Here's to Hitler, the

son of a bitch. May his pecker drop off from the seven-year itch. May they beat on his balls with a nine-pound hammer, 'til his asshole whistles The Star-Spangled Banner!"

"A litany of hate!" gasped the OKW man at the foot of the bed. "I was right. It was an assassination mission and the British were in on it! Wait until Berlin hears about *this!* Skorzeny has been begging for a crack at Eisenhower, but Himmler has been holding off from such an operation!"

"I'm not sure that's the answer," said Steiner, "but we'd better pass it on. We can't take chances with Der Fuhrer's life, and I'll be damned if I can get anything else out of him. He can't be broken while he's awake, and he only gives us nonsense under drugs. We'd better alert Berchtesgaden *and* our people in Italy. Those OSS men were headed one place or the other!"

Two Persons noticed the stars were not spinning so fast now, and the voices were fading away in the distance. Somewhere in the Medicine Lodge, a door slammed, and Two Persons remembered how he'd broken his leg. He called out, "Jump, you motherfuckers! We're spinning in!" and his grandfather said, "Go back to sleep, Dog Soldier. You have done well. I am sorry I ever laughed at you. Your medicine is stronger than your enemies and you have earned a rest before they kill you."

○○○

Sergeant Conti heard the automobile engine long before
he saw the staff car coming up the road. He saw it was
alone and hoped it was headed somewhere else. But it
slowed and stopped at the gate of Kellermann's farm,
and the driver got out to lift the pole gate aside. There
were three people in the car. Their heads were blurs at
this range. The car started up again and vanished from
sight in the trees to Conti's left. He started to rise. But
resisted the impulse. The guys at the house would have
to deal with the occupants. His job was to stay right where
he was and make certain the Krauts were alone. He
started to pump the bolt of his carbine. But resisted that
unthinking impulse too. There was a round in the chamber
and the gun was on full automatic. He had to stay cool.
This was no time to jump up and run around like a chicken
with its head cut off.

A cricket chirped behind him, and Trooper Blanchard
flopped at his side to whisper, "What's up, sarge?" I
heard a fucking car!"

Conti's conversational tone surprised even him as he said, "Get back to your position, Blanchard. Sergeant Compton will take the jerks in the car. Make sure nobody else is coming and don't leave your position again unless you have something to report!"

"I don't hear no shooting," said Blanchard. "They must be in range of Compton by now!"

"That's *his* problem. *Yours* is watching them fucking woods. Move it out, Blanchard. That's an order!"

Blanchard did as he was told, and despite himself, Conti missed his company as soon as he found himself alone again. It was a problem as old as the sling and arrow. Good soldiers know better than to bunch up. But it feels so lonely at safe interval. Maybe that was why they made those Hollywood war movies so dumb. The actors felt, instinctively, that men should stick together in a tight little bunch, yakking like a bunch of women. In a movie, you always knew they were going to kill the kid from Brooklyn as soon as he got separated fifty yards from his other buddies. In a real war, being close enough to another man to share a smoke was asking for wholesale Purple Hearts.

What the fuck was Compton *doing* back there by the house? Had they spotted the car coming into the farmyard in time to do *any*thing? Maybe he'd better have a look. Compton didn't know his ass from his elbow and . . . "Easy!" he muttered aloud. "There were only three Krauts in the car. You'd be hearing shots if the guys in Compton's stick were caught with their pants down. Just do your job and watch the fucking road, old buddy!"

A quarter mile away, Sergeant Compton peered through the lace curtains of an upstairs window and asked, "What are those Krauts yelling about, Krinke?"

Trooper Krinke stared down at the car, parked between the house and the barn, and said, "The guy that just got out wants to know where everybody is, sarge. Maybe if we just lay low, they'll go away."

Compton said, "Maybe if the dog hadn't stopped to shit, it would have caught the rabbit. We've gotta *take* them, Krinke. You have any ideas?"

"I'll send one of the Russians out to invite them in."

"You think we can trust those workers? The old man says they volunteered to work in Germany, and if the guy we sent should tip them off . . ."

"He'd be doing it with my carbine trained on his ass, and I could sort of point that out to him, sarge."

"I don't think we should try anything cute. The Russian could tip them off some way, and they could drive off as if they didn't know the score. We'd never know if they were coming back with a zillion guys until it was too late. I think we'd better just step out and tell them they've been captured."

"*You* step out and tell them, sarge! That guy down there is wearing an SS uniform. They say some SS guys act sort of frantic at times and . . ."

"So send one of the Russians. Tell him to tell the Krauts we have them covered from the house and barn. Give them, oh, thirty seconds to come out with their hands up. I won't really open up until they try to start the fucking car."

Down in the yard, Major Konrad Unger leaned out the back window and said to his driver, "There's nobody home, Martin. We must try again another time!"

SS Trooper Martin Holzheim said, "I don't understand it, Mein Herr. I told old Kellermann we were coming for that side of veal today. He promised he'd have it ready for us, and ach, I see one of Kellermann's Russians is coming out of the house. I wonder what could have kept him so long."

Holzheim put a thoughtful hand on the holster of his Walther, and the Russian, Boris, grinned. He stopped a few feet from the car and said, "You are my prisoner, pigfucker! I give you to my count of ten before I let the Americans kill you!"

"Have you been drinking again, Boris?" asked the driver. Then a curtain moved, and he glanced up warily, to stare into the muzzle of a gun barrel pointed at him from the window. The SS trooper moved his hand away from his side and called out, "Herr Major! We seem to be trapped! What are your orders?"

Major Unger leaned out, looked the way his driver was pointing with his chin, and saw the gun barrel. Across the yard, a hay-loft door slid open over the barn door. Unger swore softly, opened the door on his side, and got out. He turned to the woman still seated in the car and said, "We seem to have blundered into something, my dear. You'd better get out while I have a talk with them."

The Russian said, "Put your hands up, Nazi!" and Unger ignored him to help the woman from the car. She was a blonde of about thirty and wore the uniform of a German military nurse. She looked frightened and Unger soothed, "Easy, Sister Alfrieda. Don't let them see you're afraid."

The kitchen door opened again, and a pair of very dirty-looking young men in American battle dress came out of the house, holding carbines loosely in their hands. Unger heaved a sigh of relief and said, "They're Americans, God be thanked! I was afraid we'd run into some crazy guerrilla operation here!"

Sister Alfrieda whispered, "They look so savage!"

But Unger said, "Be calm and let me do the talking."

He smiled at Sergeant Compton and saluted, saying, "I am Major Unger, who are you?" in perfect English.

Compton smiled and said, "You speak English? Good. I'm Compton, Eighty-second Airborne. You people are our prisoners. You'd better get inside. Krinke?"

"Yeah, sarge?"

"You'd better run that staff car into the barn and get

it out of sight. Then send a runner to Conti and tell them we've got it under control. He must be sweating bullets about now."

Compton pointed at Holzheim with his gun muzzle and told Unger, "Have your buddy unbuckle his gunbelt and let the whole thing drop. Where's *your* sidearm, major?"

Unger smiled sheepishly and said, "I hardly thought I needed to carry a gun, buying groceries in the middle of Germany. But we live and learn, nicht wahr?"

He turned to his driver and told him to drop his gunbelt. The SS trooper unbuckled his belt sullenly, then held it out to Krinke, saying, "A German soldier's weapon never touches the ground, while he still lives."

Krinke took the gun belt, resisting an impulse to prove the creep wrong. There was no real reason to throw the poor slob's gunbelt in that nearby manure pile, and it made a nice souvenir. Krinke asked in German, "Are your keys in the ignition?" and Holzheim said, "Look for yourself, Ami!"

Krinke knew the meaning of the pun. Ami could be short for American, or it could mean a poor beggar in German. He decided to let it go. The slob was probably showing off for the dame. He'd talk to him about his manners later, when he didn't have an audience.

Krinke got in the car while Compton and the Russian escorted the three prisoners into the house. Momma Kellermann greeted them in the kitchen with, "There was no way we could warn you. Since last night they have held us here, and they won't let me put on my shoes!"

Compton told Unger, "You'll have to translate for me until Krinke comes in from the barn, major. Have your man and the lady sit down at the table there, and ask the old woman to fix you some coffee and cake or something. You're going to have to stay here a little while."

The nurse said, "Please, I can a little English speak.

You must not me hold a prisoner. I am Red Cross. You understand Red Cross?"

Compton nodded and said, "Yeah, and I never *liked* the mothers much! They charge more than the PX for them cigarettes that were supposed to be free. So just sit down and shut up, honey. Nobody's going noplace until the captain decides what to do about you Krauts."

Unger frowned and said, "Your leader is a captain, young man? What rank do you hold, if I may ask?"

"Buck sergeant. What's it to you?"

"Under the rules of war, I am entitled to the privileges of my rank. You will please address me as major, instead of Kraut."

Compton laughed incredulously and asked, "Am I supposed to salute you too?"

"Those are the rules among civilized military men, sergeant. My trooper and I are your prisoners for the moment. But we are entitled to respect, and as for Sister Alfrieda here, you have no right to hold *her* at all! She is under the protection of the Geneva Convention, as a noncombatant."

Compton shrugged and said, "I saw some of your Geneva Convention shit, over in East London, Kraut. You guys blew the shit out of the Geneva Conventions *and* the East End. Girl I know lost her whole fucking family to your civilized warfare."

Unger shrugged and said, "We too can tell such stories. In Hamburg was an orphanage run by the Catholic Sisters of Mercy. Would you like to hear about 300 babies roasted to death in their cribs? Or should we speak of your high-altitude strike on Hanau? There was no air-raid warning and the bombs came down during the morning rush hour. I knew a girl who lost her family too, sergeant. The girl, herself, only lost both legs."

He looked away and added, "She was my sister."

Compton shrugged and said, "The old woman's a good

cook, and we gave her plenty of the coffee we brought with us. Why don't you ask her to fix something for you and the lady, major?"

Unger nodded and said, "Thank you, sergeant. May I ask when this captain of yours is due back?"

"Anytime now," said Compton, turning to another trooper in the room to say, "Keep your eye on them, Mike. I'm going to check with the other guys."

Major Unger waited until he'd left and said in German, "Play up to them, Sister Alfrieda. The Anglo-Saxon mind is unable to sustain a cold rage. If you can only get an Englishman or American smiling back at you, the rest is simple. They are only dangerous when they are frowning."

Martin Holzheim asked, "When do we make our move, Herr Major?"

Unger said, "When I figure one out. Meanwhile, keep that Bavarian temper of yours under control. I shall tell you when it's time to prove your basic superiority, son."

The trooper guarding them frowned and said, "Talk English, major. I don't like it when people whisper in Kraut together, see?"

Unger smiled and said, "We were just deciding what we wanted to eat. But you are the boss here. Dare I ask the old woman for some coffee and cake."

"Sure, go ahead," said the trooper, relaxing a bit.

Unger turned to Frau Kellermann and said, "We would like anything you care to serve, gracious lady." Then, still smiling at the farmer's wife, he continued in German, "There, you see how simple it is? Just keep *smiling* at the bastards until I give the word!"

○○○

Oberst Von Dreihausen read the report on his desk
when he got to the underground OKW office and snorted
in disbelief. The Paris office couldn't expect anyone to
take such nonsense seriously. It was known the people at
SHAEF frowned on political assassination. British intelligence had done some rude things through partisans and
paid international scoundrels. But the OSS did not send
men in uniform to assassinate. At least, they never had
up to now. . . .

He picked up one of the phones on his desk, pushed a
button, and snapped, "Von Dreihausen. Somebody is
crazy. I don't know if it's Steiner or the Americans. But
we'd better follow up on that story about American paratroopers in British bombers. What have we got so far?"

"Just the rumor our informant picked up in the Norwich pub, Herr Oberst. Wait. I have one more item. Two
of the British planes returned from wherever they went.
One failed to come back. We have a man working at the

British airdrome. He heard them talking about it in the NAAFI canteen."

"Is that all he heard, damn it? Contact him and tell him to find out more!"

"I can contact him, Herr Oberst. But there is nothing he can tell us. The crews of both British planes have been sent to London under guard. All the ground crews know is that they flew across the Channel last night. Security was very tight."

"Do we know when they took off and, more important, when they returned?"

"Yes, Herr Oberst. They took off at midnight. Returned about 0800. The crews went directly to London with no discussion of the plane that never came back. The enlisted men at the base talked about it amongst themselves, of course. But nobody there seems to know just what happened."

"Contact our London branch and report back to me as soon as you have anything. Tell our people in London to get out there and *work,* damn it! We didn't send them there to drink Whitbread's."

Von Dreihausen slammed down the receiver, got up, and went to the wall map across the room. He took a length of string and a grease pencil, measured off the four-hour range of a Mosquito, and holding one end of the string in the position of Norwich, drew a compass circle with the red grease pencil from the Baltic to the Adriatic Seas. He stepped back and studied his handiwork. Then he cursed. Nearly everything in Occupied Europe fit inside the circle he'd just drawn. Der Fuhrer's headquarters at Berchtesgaden, parts of Yugoslavia, and the north of Italy fit equally well as the probable target. If the damned bombers had circled or dog-legged about *inside* the circle, the bastards could have landed almost *anywhere!*

He went back to the desk, picked up the phone, and

pushed another button. A husky voice said, "Here speaks Borman."

"Von Dreihausen here, General Borman. I do not wish to alarm you. But there may be an attempt on Der Fuhrer's life afoot. Tell me, is he at his home in Berchtesgaden?"

"Never mind where Der Fuhrer is. What's this all about, Herr Oberst?"

"We're holding an American paratrooper in Lyons. He seems to be a member of some OSS mission that might, just might, be on its way to Berchtesgaden."

"Have him brought to Berlin. I'll get some of Himmler's people to question him!"

Von Dreihausen hesitated before he asked, "Do you think that is wise, Herr General? The man has been co-operating, more or less, with *our* people and . . ."

"I know what you think of Himmler's methods. But they get fast results. You will send this American to Berlin, Herr Oberst. That is an order!"

ooo

Dave Evans, Matt Price, and the two others got back about an hour after the three Germans had been captured. Sergeant Compton stepped outside to fill him in on the prisoners. The captain went over to the barn and checked out the car before entering the house. He asked Corporal Muller, "What do you think those numbers on the bumper mean, Muller?"

The German-speaking noncom answered, "Hard to say, sir. Probably a unit code and a motor pool number, the same as on our vehicles."

"Look around and see if you can find some paint you can mix well enough to pass for that blotchy camouflage. They'll miss that car in a while. Do we have a sign painter among the men?"

"I'll ask, sir. But what are we supposed to replace those letters with?"

"I'm not sure it matters. I've never been able to make heads nor tails out of the numbers and letters on *our* jeeps. Just change the paint job a little. I don't want anyone to recognize this particular car if they see it."

Muller asked, "Who's going to see it here in this barn, sir?"

Evans said, "Change the paint job. I may be taking it out for a spin this afternoon."

He turned to go back to the house. Price, who'd overheard the exchange, asked, "What's the plan, mate? We can't crowd your whole lot in that one ruddy staff car! How many of us *are* there, anyway?"

"Twenty-two, thanks to that bad break Yellowpony's stick had. Sixteen troopers, two corporals, two sergeants, you, and me. I make that twenty-two."

"Too little and too many," sighed Price. "We've too few men to fight off a ruddy German platoon. Too many to fade into the countryside. You did say you were Cymreag, didn't you?"

"*Com what?*"

"*Welsh,* man! You and me are both from The Valley!"

"What's that supposed to mean, Price?"

"It means we ought to hang together, Dai Evans! You and me and the two lads who speak German could go a long way in yon motor car. If we took those prisoners' uniforms and found some other kit the farmer's sons may have left about the house. . . ."

"Negative," said Evans. "We all get out together or *none* of us make it. I'm getting an idea about that staff car, Price. But we're not running out on anybody."

Evans led the way to the house and went inside. As the captain entered, Major Unger and his driver jumped up from the table and snapped to attention. Evans returned the SS officer's salute with a half-hearted wave of his hand an said, "As you were, major. I understand you speak English?"

"I studied it at the university, captain. Dare I speak out for this lady your men unlawfully detain?"

Evans stared down morosely at the nurse, who'd remained seated at the table. He said, "Tell her none of my men will molest her."

The nurse said, "Please, your soldiers have been most correct."

Unger smiled at Evans and said, "You have no right to hold Sister Alfrieda here. Under the rules of civilized warfare, you must let her go."

Across the room, Krinke whistled a few bars of "It Seems to Me I've Heard That Song Before." Evans said, "If the three of you behave yourselves, I'll let all of you go when we're through here."

"But as a point of international law . . ." began the German.

"If one of you gets out of line," Evans cut in, "I'll kill all three of you. So that makes *you* responsible for the lady's safety, major. Do you understand what I am saying?"

"Yes, captain. But under protest."

"Protest all you like. But don't make any sudden moves. Now, what brought you to this farm?"

Unger shrugged and said, "The old man in the other room had a side of veal to sell. Sister Alfrieda wanted it for her mess."

Evans nodded down at the woman and asked, "Are you in charge of rations at the hospital, sister?"

Sister Alfrieda missed the warning look Unger shot her as she answered, "Please, the food is for the children. We have been so short of food that I thought . . ."

Evans cut in, "Children? You mean those Jewish children at the concentration camp?"

Unger said, "They are well treated, captain. Despite what you may have heard."

Evans nodded and said, "Oh, you're a cute one, aren't you, major. Asking me to turn loose an SS nurse!"

Sister Alfrieda protested, "Please, Herr Hauptman, I

am in charge of little children only. I am, how do you say, a medic?"

Evans said, "Never mind. What I said before still stands. Now look——I want you to think about what I am asking before you give me any tricky answers. You have my word you'll all be set free, unharmed, when we're ready to leave. But if anyone comes looking for you, I can promise you'll die before we do. So tell it to me straight. How long do we have before the three of you are missed?"

Unger shrugged and said, "I can say truthfully that I do not know. I am the camp commandant. Since rank has its privileges, my comings and goings are not questioned."

"Is this dame your girlfriend?"

The German lowered his eyes and said, "If you please, I am a married man."

Evans said, "I didn't ask you that. I asked you if this broad is more than a nurse to you, or more important, do your men *think* she is?"

Sister Alfrieda blushed and said, "Please, the major has always been most correct with me. But naturlich, there is always such talk about officers and any woman."

Evans nodded and said, "That figures. So let's hope they think the two of you left for a nice long drive in the country. What time do you absolutely have to be back, major? Remember, your life may depend on a right answer."

Unger said, "It is to be expected that the commandant be there when the flag is lowered for the night."

Evans glanced at his wrist and said, "It's twenty after ten. What time do you guys hold retreat?"

"The flag is lowered at 5:00 P.M. That is when the officer of the day takes over for the night. Guard mount and the reading of orders comes at the same time. I am always there at such times as the reading of orders and the lowering of our banner."

Evans mused, "That gives us a good six hours before

you three are missed. If I know anything about any army, your second in command will cover for you as long as he can, thinking you're off somewhere with your girl. They should start thinking about looking for you a little after dark. They'll start with a few discreet phone calls. But by nine or ten tonight, they'll start sending people out to look for you. How many men do you have at that camp, major?"

"Two hundred and fifty. How many have you?"

"You let me worry about that. You guys use diamond patrols, don't you?"

"You mean one man out on point, two out on flank, and one covering the rear, with the leader in the center? That is the usual form in any army. They will, of course, send out more than one such patrol, once we are missed."

"Okay. Your second in command can't spare more than fifty on his first sweep. If they don't stumble over us, he'll get on the horn and ask for help. What are the odds they'll search for you here?"

Unger shook his head and said, "I don't know. We are not that far from the camp. They will surely inquire at every farm within a ten kilometer radius."

"So we have to be on our way by ten at the latest. We'd better get the show on the road."

He looked around at the crowded kitchen and said, "There's too much confusion here. Krinke?"

"Yessir?"

"You just made Corporal. Take two men from each of the sergeants and form a guard detail. One man at a time takes a break for chow or piss call. Four out of the five of you on duty at all times. I don't want the prisoners together in the kitchen like this. Take them upstairs. Have you shaken down all the rooms up there?"

"Yessir. Four dormer rooms on one side of the hall. Storage on the other. Empty crawl space in the peak of the roof."

"Okay. The women go in the bigger bedroom. The

farmer and this driver in the boys' room. Major Unger
is to be kept alone in the guest room farthest from the
stairs. All doors to be left open. Two men at the head of
the stairs. Two at the far end. One of you walks back
and forth along the hall. When anyone takes a break,
reshuffle so that there's always two on the stairs."

Krinke frowned and asked, "May I make a suggestion,
sir?"

"Go ahead, Corporal."

"We might wind up with a crossfire situation with men
at each end of the hall, sir."

"Good thinking. How do you want to work it, Krinke?"

"Couple of guys at the head of the stairs, one guy
walking the hall, two outside, keeping an eye on the windows. It's only a two-story drop and . . ."

"I like it. Have them cover the windows from the barn.
That way they'll be out of sight and can act as lookouts
too. Do it your way and get these people off my back,
Corporal Krinke."

Major Unger got to his feet and protested, "I wish to
have my driver with me, captain. Holzheim is a personal
servant, and under the rules of war, he belongs with me!"

Evans shot him a weary look and said, "You'll do as
Corporal Krinke says, or he'll blow your head off. Those
are the rules of war I just made up. I want you all upstairs on the double. Move!"

Krinke said, "Macht schnell!" and waved the muzzle of
his carbine toward the stairwell, adding in English, "Rogers
and O'Connor, let's fall in. We'll get the guys from Conti's
stick after we've bedded these Krauts down up there."

Matt Price waited until the kitchen had cleared before
he went to the chair Unger had vacated and sank down
wearily. He looked up at Evans and asked, "Why are you
mucking about with the five of them? You know what has
to be done. We'll have to liquidate the Russians too before
we leave."

Evans shot him a warning look and said, "Compton, I want you guys and these Russians in the front parlor for now."

He waited until he and Price were alone in the kitchen before he asked, "Have you gone crazy? Those Russians might speak some English!"

"They don't. I asked. They think we're taking them with us when we leave."

Evans said, "We can't. What was that shit about killing everybody?"

"You've no other choice, Yank. It's a full night's march to the Swiss frontier and only seven perishing miles to the nearest phone. Besides, there's no telling how much they know about this mission. Your lads have been talking to them all this time, and anyone might have overhead anything. It's simple, when you think about it. We just can't leave anyone behind, alive. It can't be done clean and nice like. They've already tied one hand behind our backs by forbidding us to just blow the perishing place up. If you let those ruddy prisoners live, you're tying *both* bloody hands!"

"We'll cross that bridge when we come to it. Right now, I have an idea how we can smuggle you into the hydrogenation plant."

He outlined what he proposed to do as Price stared at him with an expression of disbelief. When Evans had finished, he shook his head and said, "Christ on a fucking bicycle! To think you just said *I* was crazy!"

"I'll admit it's a bit wild," said Evans, "but I can't think of a better way, and if it works . . ."

"You'll need that Krinke bloke too. Has to be at least two lads speaking German if it's to work at all."

"You like the idea?"

"I think it's bloody awful. But it's better than anything *I* can come up with!"

The neatly typed translation reached MI5 a little before noon. The British intelligence officer at the liaison desk read it and picked up a phone. He reached his American opposite number at SHAEF and said, "Bentley, here. We just got a report from the FFI. They say one of your chaps is being sent to Berlin this aft. He seems to be one of that lot from Operation Octane. He bailed out over Lyons, and a French agent working in the Luftwaffe hospital's been keeping an eye on him."

The American G2 man said, "Christ! He must have spilled his guts by now!"

Bentley said, "I don't think so. The French were quite glowing in their report. Seems the chap's a Red Indian named Yellowpony. He was badly injured in the landing. But he's held up under torture and Scopolamine so far. He gave the Jerries some wild story about an assassination mission aimed at Berchtesgaden, and they're in hell's own flap at the moment."

"Is he the only one captured?"

"Yes. His plane was fouled in a barrage balloon and blew to bits when it hit the ground. I daresay they were carrying explosives. The Jerries have recovered some ID tags, but that's about all. They know it was some sort of combined op, but nothing else. What do you think we should do about Yellowpony?"

"We can't let the Krauts keep him. Sooner or later, he's got to talk."

"That's the way I see it. He's done for if he reaches Berlin. Himmler's chaps are quite good at getting information out of any prisoner."

"You say we have somebody at the hospital that can get to him?"

"Yes, a ward attendant they think is a collaborator from Alsace. He more or less has the run of the hospital with his buckets and mop."

The American intelligence operator thought for a time. Then he sighed and said, "I guess we'd better ask the FFI to make sure he never reaches Berlin alive. Do you have the poor slob's full name? I'd better take it down."

Bentley said, "It's Joseph Yellowpony. He refused to give his rank or unit."

"That's close enough," said the G2 man. "I'll check it out and see that he's written up for a posthumous Silver Star."

○○

The German guards at the main gate were arguing about the football matches when they saw the staff car coming down the road. One of them said, "I still say Gunther is the best kicker in the All Services League, goddamn your eyes!"

His companion answered, "He's past his prime. But we'll talk about it later. After we see what those fucking SS men want here."

The car braked to a stop, it's engine running, and a young man wearing a silver skull on his black and silver hat stuck his head out to yell, "Open up, the major, here, is in a hurry!"

The nearest guard stepped over to the car, saying, "The workers you sent over this morning just left, sir."

Corporal Muller, sitting on the passenger's side in Major Unger's uniform, snapped, "Open the damned gate. We have civilian technicians here to check out a sabotage report!"

"Sabotage? . . ."

"Jump! You are holding up the war! What is your name, soldier?"

"Dorfler, Airman Third Class, Herr Major! I am sorry, Herr Major, but we have our orders. . . ."

"I order you to open that damned gate. I'll take full responsibility for these technicians. We didn't have time to type up authorization. We have to get to those boilers right away!"

"May I have your name, sir?"

"Unger, Konrad, SS Major. Check it out with your sergeant of the guard. But open that damned gate!"

The Luftwaffe guard nearest the car motioned to his comrade, who slid the gate aside and shot the coverall-clad men in the rear seat a worried look as the car zoomed past. He slid the gate shut again and said, "You should have insisted on seeing their authorization, Hans." But his comrade shrugged and said, *"You* get on the wrong side of a field-grade SS man if you want, kid. I just do as I'm told. We'll tell the sarge when he comes by and let *him* argue with the son of a bitch!"

"He won't be back for at least an hour. The sarge was just here, remember?"

"What do you expect *me* to do about it, damn it?"

"Maybe I'd better run over to the guardhouse and tell the lieutenant?"

"You can't leave me here alone. Fire three shots and let the lieutenant come to us, if you're that worried about it."

The guard started to unsling his rifle. Then he shrugged and said, "We'd better wait. Maybe the sarge will come by before they leave. What was that name he gave?"

"Unger. I think I know the name. He's in charge of those Jews from the concentration camp."

From the rear seat of the staff car, Captain Evans said, "Swing right at that next turn, Krinke. Pull in behind that thing that looks like a locomotive standing on its head!"

Krinke said, "Yessir." Then he laughed a bit wildly and said, "You sure pulled your rank on those Krauts, Muller!"

Muller, pale as death, squeaked, "I thought I was going to shit in my pants! Chesus, I'm glad my grandma slapped some German into me."

Krinke said, "Why do I know any fucking Kraut? I wish I was a fucking 4F." He braked to a stop between the retorts and the catalytic chamber.

Evans opened the door on his side and said, "You stay in the seat and keep the engine running, Krinke. Muller, you'd better get out and stand around as scenery in case anyone comes."

Price got out, went around to the trunk, and opened it. He said, "Help me with this gear, Yank. I have to work fast and it's not like I was a perishing mule, you know."

Evans and Price unloaded the things Price had brought from the house. They included tools he'd found at the Kellermann farm. He said, "Up those metal stairs to the first level, Yank." Without waiting for an answer, he started for the catalytic machinery. Corporal Muller began to pace up and down, his feet feeling small and loose in the size thirteen boots. Around his waist, he'd strapped the sidearm of the Nazi driver. The captain had shown him how a German Walther fired. But he'd never been very good with any pistol. Muller felt naked without his carbine. He heard a metallic clang and looked up. He couldn't see what they were doing up there. The captain and that Limey were lost in that maze of pipes and valves. They said the Limey knew how all that garbage worked. He swept his eyes beyond, to a looming cracking tower, and muttered, "Shit, there must be a million miles of pipes and valves in this dump! How can anyone ever keep track of all them valves?"

Up on the platform, Evans asked, "What are you doing?"

Price gave the nail another tap before he answered, "This is a pressure relief plug. Special alloy that melts and releases this spring-loaded valve if this line gets too hot. By driving a nail in through the soft alloy . . ."

"I get it. The steel nail won't melt. It'll hold the spring in place while the pressure builds up enough to blow a joint somewhere else."

Price nodded and said, "The nail acts as a heat sink too."

He took something from his pocket and started rubbing it on the dimly visible nail head. Evans asked what it was and Price said, "Silver crayon. Blends the nail head in with the alloy. They'll see a perfectly sound alloy plug the first couple of times they check. Now, let's see what we can do with this ruddy thermodial!"

He unscrewed the back of the dial as Evans watched, impressed by the skill of the Welshman's strong stubby fingers. Price had the touch of a surgeon. Or perhaps, the touch of a man who'd managed to keep all ten fingers learning to handle explosives. Price took the back off, reached into bend a spring, and muttered, "There, she's two hundred and, ah, thirty-two degrees off. They'll spot that, of course. But they'll think it's metal fatigue and it will keep their ruddy minds off yon pressure relief valve. You always muck things up in triplicate, you see. Gives them two out of three chances to be wrong."

He loosened a screw on a third valve, said, "That does it here. Let's move on to the bloody gas line!"

Down in the alleyway below them, Muller spotted a man in coveralls coming toward their stolen car. He walked to meet the man, who asked in German, "What's going on? We don't have any of your Jews working here this afternoon."

"Who the devil are you?" snapped Muller officiously.

The man in the coveralls said, "I'm Gottlieb, from the maintenance office. I'm *supposed* to be here!"

Muller nodded curtly, pretending to be Eric Von Stroheim in *Twelve Graves to Cairo,* and said, "So? I am SS Major Unger. I have some technicians up there, checking out a sabotage report from OKW."

"Does the front office know of this? I'd better go and get the director!"

The man turned away and Muller sighed, "I was afraid you'd say a dumb thing like that!" Then he lunged forward, judo-chopped the German across the back of the neck, and sent him crashing to the cinder-covered ground. Muller jumped high in the air, came down hard with his heels in the small of the fallen man's back, and broke his spine.

Krinke opened the door on his side and Muller snapped, "Back inside and keep that fucking motor running! I'll get rid of him!"

Muller looked around, saw his improvisation had gone unobserved, and bent down to grab the dead man's ankles. He dragged the German to the rear of the car, opened the trunk, and manhandled his victim into it. The German's body was like an empty sack of potatoes, and Muller grimaced as his hands touched the wet seat of his coveralls. He slammed the trunk lid shut, went around to Krinke's open window, and said, "Remember we never saw him, should anybody ask."

Krinke said, "We can't drive out with a dead Kraut in the trunk! What if they stop us for a search?"

"If they stop us, we're already in trouble. That stiff might stop a few bullets for us as we go out! Just keep her ready to roll while I watch for other nosey Nazis!"

Unaware of what had happened down below, Matt Price was saying, "This elbow joint's what I was looking for. Hand me that brace and bit, Yank!"

Price lay on his back on the metal catwalk as Evans

gave him the tool. Price started drilling up into the bottom of the eight-inch, insulated gas pipe and Evans asked, "How long is this liable to take us?"

Price, grimacing as asbestos fibers fell in his sweaty face, said, "Four, five minutes, give or take what sort of steel they have under this ruddy shit. Diamond bit will bite through anything, in time. Pick up that brass fitting I attached to the tubing and have it ready."

Evans knelt, picked up the coil of what looked like copper wire, and uncoiled one end. The copper was ultra-fine eighth-inch tubing. The bore was less than a sixteenth. But a very small amount of pure oxygen would do terrible things to the hot catalyst grids inside the gently purring chamber. The fitting Price had threaded to the end was only a little wider and looked like a tire valve. Evans had only a hazy idea how it worked. There was another just like it at the other end of the tubing. The coil was two feet in diameter and it hardly seemed possible it would reach as far as it had to. He sincerely hoped Price knew what he was doing.

Evans looked at his watch and couldn't believe they'd been inside the plant less than ten minutes. It felt more like a couple of hours.

There was a sudden piercing hiss, and Price crabbed sideways, snapping, "Quick, the fitting!"

Evans placed the end of the tubing in the hand Price held out, and the Welshman moved like a cat, pulling out the drill bit as he popped the fitting in the hole against the pressure of the screaming hot gas. There was an audible click, the gas stopped hissing, and Price clapped a hand to his mouth, moaning in pain.

Evans gasped, "Are you hurt?"

Price shook his head. He sucked his blistered fingers for a moment. Then grinned weakly and said, "The jet didn't touch me. But the stuff's hotter than molten lead. The bloody brass heated up before I could let go!"

Evans started to touch the coil. But Price knocked his hand aside, saying, "Don't! It's almost hot enough to melt by now. Copper conducts heat, you know!"

Price took a notched screwdriver and a pair of asbestos gloves from inside his coveralls. He put on the gloves, gingerly uncoiled a few feet of the tubing, and still lying on his back, started pressing the copper line into the soft insulation of the gas pipe. He muttered, "This is the tricky part. I have to get it deep enough in the insulation to be hidden without crimping it shut with this ruddy tool!"

"You'll never reach the oxygen tanks with that tubing!" Evans protested.

But Price said, "I don't have to. You see that green pipe down on the next level? That's an ox pipe running to another part of the plant. It has nothing to do with this chamber. So there's no reason for them to notice the few feet of bare tubing we have to connect to it. The hard part's drilling through the bloody ox pipe. It's thick, high-pressure steel tubing."

Evans glanced at his watch and asked, "How *long*, Price? We've been here almost a quarter of an hour!"

"I need at least another twenty minutes, and I never wanted to *be* here in the *first* flaming place!"

Evans crawled over to the edge and looked down. He spotted Muller and the car below and said, "Nobody's questioned us so far. But for Christ's sake, *hurry!*"

Price said, "Take it easy, Yank. Unless I do this right, there ain't no reason to be doing it at all!"

ooo

The sergeant of the guard rode up to the main gate on his bicycle and put a leg down to steady himself as he asked the men on duty, "Is all in order here?"

One of the guards said, "I think so. Do you know a Major Unger from the SS?"

"Of course. He's the commandant at the concentration camp up the valley. What about him?"

"He's an arrogant son of a bitch for one thing. He just drove in like he owned the damned place!"

"He's in charge of security in the area. What did he want?"

"Something about those Jews of his. He had some technicians with him. Said they had to look at something inside."

"Where did he go, the office?"

"I guess so. He's probably giving the director a bad time. He certainly is a *mean* bastard!"

The sergeant shrugged and said, "Those SS men think their shit don't stink."

132

The guard named Dorfler said, "He took my name, sarge. I think he's going to put me on report."

"Good God, what did you say to him?"

"Nothing. I just asked him what he wanted and he started threatening me. He took my name down, and if he gives it to the captain, I can kiss my leave good-bye for this year!"

The sergeant said, "He was probably just throwing his rank around. I don't think he'll turn you in, and if he does, I'll stand up for you."

"Against an SS major? You'll only get *yourself* in trouble, sarge!"

The sergeant thought a moment. Then he said, "Open the gate. I'll run over to the office and make myself useful. Maybe if I suck up to the bastard, he'll forget to put you on report."

○○

Matt Price blew on his hands and said, "Coo, if you don't burn your bloody fingers off, you freeze them! That oxygen's fucking *cold*. But I think that does it here."

Evans nodded approvingly at the inconspicuous tap the Welshman had fitted to the green pipe and asked, "Why didn't you wear the gloves while you drilled it, Price?"

Price said, "Had to feel what I was about. Just let me rub a bit of lampblack over the fitting and we'll move over to the cracking towers."

Evans watched Price rub the new look out of the small shiny fitting and marveled, "It hardly seems possible that little gadget can do the damage you say, Price."

Price shrugged and said, "It's secondary school chemistry, Yank. Hydrocarbon compounds burn because carbon has a thirst for oxygen. Feed carbon monoxide one extra atom of oxygen and it never wants to burn again."

"What's going on in the chamber, right now?"

"It's heating up for one thing. The catalyst grids are slowly burning out. Parts of the process are still going

134

on. We're only bleeding a *bit* of ox into it, after all. But while most of the gas is condensing to synthetic oil, a tenth or more is turning to carbon char. A fine black dust about like graphite. It's sooting up the inside of the chamber and dropping like pitch black snow in the condensing oil. They won't notice anything until it gets over to the cracking towers to be distilled into its proper fractions."

Evans grinned and said, "I can see what happens next. The crud should gum the whole works when it starts to settle out of the oil. But won't they still be getting clean fractions off at the top trays?"

"They will for a few days, as the carbon char slowly coats the hot metal and clogs up the vapor openings. Then they'll shut the towers down and clean them, wondering how in bleeding hell they got so dirty. They ought to have to clean out the towers more than once before yon catalytic chamber burns out. When *that* happens, they'll have to shut down the whole flaming plant!"

Evans looked at his watch and said, "Jesus, first this thing was running slow and now it's running fast. How long do you need to place those dummy charges under the cracking towers?"

"Depends on how many perishing Jerries they have mucking about over there. This part of the plant more or less runs on its own. But you have to monitor cracking towers. Could be a wait until the coast is clear for a few mos."

Evans gathered up the tools they'd brought and moved over to the steps as Price followed. Evans got to the ground and moved around the brickwork base to where he'd left the others and the car. Muller said, "We had a little problem, captain." But Evans snapped, "Tell me on the way," and went directly to the car. He opened the trunk to throw the tools in and jumped back, gasping, "Jesus H. Christ!"

Muller said, "That was the problem, sir. I didn't know

where else to *put* the motherfucker!"

Evans threw the tools in with the grinning corpse and slammed the lid shut, asking, "Are you sure he was alone, Muller?"

Muller said, "Yessir. I tried to talk to the slob. But he started acting suspicious."

Price came over and Evans said, "Pile in. We have to get to the cracking towers and *out* before they miss that worker!"

Evans got in, himself, and told Krinke, "Turn toward the canal at that service road ahead."

As the car started up, a trio of workers came around one corner of the coal retort. The workers glanced over in idle curiosity as the car passed them and Krinke said, "Jesus, that was timing it close!"

Evans said, "Just remember you're a hotshot SS man and drive like you knew where you're going. It's going smooth as silk!"

Beside him, Matt Price muttered, "Too bloody smooth to last." But then he added, "I see the cracking towers up ahead. Let's place our charges and get our arses *out* of here!"

❍❍❍

The plant director stared at the Luftwaffe sergeant in the outer office and frowned as he asked, "You say Major Unger is in this plant? I don't understand it. He always comes here to the office when he visits us."

The sergeant said, "I only know what the gate guards told me, Herr Direktor. It was something about the Jews he sent over to help with the coal shoveling."

The director nodded and said, "In that case, he must be over by the coal retorts. Do you know the way, sergeant?"

The Luftwaffe man shook his head and said, "It all looks like a plumber's nightmare to me, Herr Direktor."

The civilian looked around at the other workers in the main office and called, "Where is Gottlieb?"

A man at a drawing board looked up and answered, "He went to check the valve settings on the catalytic chamber, Herr Direktor!"

The manager nodded and said, "He's probably with the major, then. Will you show the sergeant, here, the way to that part of our installation?"

The man got up from his drawing board and said, "Come with me, sergeant. I'll take you to your officer."

"He's not *my* officer!" protested the sergeant, as he started to follow the man outside.

The technician asked, "Oh? You sound like you don't like him much!"

"I don't," said the sergeant. "He just got after one of my men for no reason at all."

The technician said, "That doesn't sound like the Major Unger *I* know. He's always been quite pleasant to me."

"Oh? How well do you know the major, then?"

"I just know him to talk to. He has some unusual views on war production, even for a party man. I don't think I'd like to be one of his Jews. But as I said, he's usually very friendly to *us*. Your guard must have caught him in a bad mood, or perhaps the man was fresh."

"Dorfler's a shy country type. He wouldn't get fresh with a *woman*, let alone an SS officer! The major must be hot under the collar about something."

They headed for the coal retorts and the technician said, "Well, let's find him and see if we can't cool him down."

ΟΟΟΟΟΟΟΟΟΟΟΟΟΟΟΟΟΟΟΟΟΟΟΟΟΟΟΟΟΟΟΟΟΟΟΟΟΟΟΟΟΟΟΟΟΟΟΟ

At the hospital near Lyons, a man in a dark civilian
suit sat on a bentwood chair by the door of Yellowpony's
room. A sign on the corridor wall said smoking was forbidden, but the man was smoking a big black cheroot.
The Geheime Staatspolizei made its own rules.

A small wiry man with steel-wool hair pushed a laundry
hamper down the corridor and stopped at Yellowpony's
door. He asked the Gestapo man, "Is this the room they
are keeping the American in?"

The Gestapo man, bored with his dull guard detail and
willing at the moment to talk about almost anything, said,
"Yes, we're waiting for transportation. RSHA is taking
the prisoner off the OKW's hands. Those army men haven't
been able to get much out of him."

The hospital attendant nodded and said, "I have to
change his linen," and started to open the door. The
Gestapo man got to his feet and said, "You can't go in
there, damn it!"

The hospital attendant answered, "What do you mean

I can't go in? How am I to change the linen from out here? I have my orders, see? You can check with Doctor Allendorf if you like!"

"I don't see why you want to change his linen now. He's leaving for Berlin in less than an hour."

"Look, does anything make sense these days? I know as well as you it's stupid. But a man can get in trouble questioning orders, nicht wahr?"

The Gestapo man hesitated. Then he shrugged and said, "Hell, I don't care what you do to the swine's linen. I have to watch you though. I have my own orders."

The ward attendant pushed the laundry hamper through the door as the Gestapo man followed. Yellowpony was conscious, his head propped up on pillows and the leg cast still in traction. The ward attendant smiled down at him and said in English, "Not one sound, if you want to live!"

Then he turned, raised the silencer-fitted target pistol in his left hand, and shot the Gestapo man just above the right eyebrow.

The German slid down the wall, a surprised look in his dead eyes, as the man in hospital whites moved quickly to the door and closed it, muttering in French, "Merde alors, the thrice-accursed gun shoots high and to the left!"

Yellowpony propped himself up on one elbow and gasped, "What the fuck's going on? Who the fuck are you?"

"Lieutenant Roche, FFI. We do not have the time for conversation, hein? How bad is that leg? Can you stand for me to lower it from the sling?"

"If you can get me out of this contraption, I can stand anything! You talk, I listen, white-eyes!"

The French agent pulled a folding wheelchair from the laundry hamper and swiftly opened it. He tucked his gun inside his hospital whites and took out a pocket knife to cut Yellowpony's leg free of the traction sling. The cast dropped and the Amerind clenched his teeth in pain. Roche shot him a concerned look and snapped, "For God's sake, don't scream!"

"Who's screaming?" grunted Yellowpony. "Help me get in the fucking wheelchair!"

"First you must put this on," said the Frenchman, taking a Luftwaffe officer's hospital robe from the hamper and helping Yellowpony into it. The Amerind sat on the edge of the bed, trying not to pass out as the blood rushed from his head and started to throb savagely in his broken leg. Roche took a roll of surgical gauze from the hamper and said, "First we get you in the chair. Then I must wrap your head in this. Remember, you are a Luftwaffe fighter pilot who's been badly burned in a crash. Do you speak any German at all?"

"Not a fucking word!"

"Ah, in that case, you must let me do the talking for you. Those terrible burns make it painful to move your lips, and you are, of course, under heavy sedation."

As Roche wrapped his head like a mummy's, Yellowpony asked, "What are you going to do with the Kraut? You can't just leave him there like that."

"First things first," said the Frenchman, pinning the end of the bandage in place and stepping back to view his improvisation.

He nodded approvingly and said, "Now, for M'sieur le Boche!"

He dropped to one knee by the man he'd assassinated, went through the dead man's clothes, and said, "Not bad. One pistol, one set of handcuffs with a key, Gestapo identification, a nice lighter, and three cigars. Our friends will find all of these most useful, if we live to reach them."

Yellowpony watched as the small but deceptively strong Frenchman rolled the corpse under the bed. Yellowpony said, "You're from the underground, huh?"

"French Forces of the Interior," Roche corrected, getting to his feet and opening the door. He looked outside, saw no one was looking, and pulled the dead man's chair inside. Then he got behind Yellowpony's wheelchair and said, "Keep your head down and act like you're half asleep. When in doubt, faint."

He wheeled the injured paratrooper out in the corridor and headed for an outside ramp. As they swung a corner, a Junoesque blonde in a nurse's uniform came out of a room, stopped, and blocked their path. Roche smiled and said in German, "Good afternoon, Sister Morgenstern."

The nurse said, "Good afternoon, Paul. What have we here?"

The FFI man said, "Crash victim. Doctor Allendorf told me to take him for a walk around the grounds. He needs fresh air."

"I thought Doctor Allendorf had left for the day, Paul."

"He has. I carried his bags to his car. His last order for the day was to take this poor fellow out for some change of scene."

The nurse reached down and took Yellowpony's wrist, saying, "Let me feel your pulse. How do you feel right now?"

Yellowpony didn't answer and the Frenchman said, "He's not quite with us today. He's under sedation and terribly depressed. I don't think he believes plastic surgery will do much for what's left of his face."

"You poor boy!" said the nurse. "I see you broke a leg too. But you're going to be just fine. Your pulse is beating strongly and . . ." She frowned down at Yellowpony's hand and mused, "My, he has quite a tan, hasn't he?"

"Italian front," explained the Frenchman, casually.

The nurse nodded and said, "Carry on, Paul. Mind you don't keep him out too long. It's a bit nippy this afternoon."

Roche nodded and wheeled Yellowpony to the end of the corridor and down a ramp to an asphalt path that wound across spacious tree-shaded grounds. Yellowpony asked, "Where are we going?"

The Frenchman explained, "To a stolen car, if we ever reach the parking lot. Some friends are waiting for us with forged documents that *say* we are taking you to the railway station for the Gestapo. If they fail to find that pig I left under your bed before the Berlin train pulls out, the confusion should prove most amusing, hein?"

"You won't be able to come back here again, will you?"

"No. Fortunately for you, I was about to leave in any case. One of the men in my resistance cell dropped out of sight this morning, and while we do not *know* he was picked up by le Boche, one does not take chances. Since I must take to the bushes in any case, I thought it only just to take you with me."

"Can you guys get me home?"

"Eventually. You shall be passed on to a sector that specializes in such matters. My sector concerns itself with making life difficult for le Boche."

Yellowpony grinned under the bandages and said, "So I noticed. You had that gun and silencer loaded for Kraut, huh?"

"Not exactly," said Roche, "But fortunately I was born an opportunist."

ooo

Dave Evans followed Price along the steel mesh catwalk and asked, "How come we're so high? I thought you were going to place the charges at ground level."

The Welshman said, "I was. But there's just no place down there they wouldn't be found in half an hour. We want Jerry to have to *look* for these charges, remember?"

He got to the side of the cracking tower facing the canal and knelt to lower a satchel charge between the inner edge of the catwalk and the riveted steel wall of the silolike hulk they'd climbed halfway to the top. He took a roll of friction tape in his free hand and started taping the charge to the steel plates as Evans stared out across the landscape. They had a clear view from here of the apple orchard they'd been hiding in a few hours ago. Was it only a few hours? It seemed more like a month!

Beyond the apple orchard and some fields on the far side, Evans saw the white roof of the German hospital. He thought a moment and told Price, "Negative on that doctored fuse idea. I want you to really set the charge to

144

blow. Can you time it for, say, twenty-four hours?"

Price said, "Of course. But we're not supposed to blow this bloody tower, Yank. I thought these charges were just to take Jerry's mind off the real reason for our visit!"

"They are. That's why they have to be set to really go off. It's not going to take them twenty-four hours to figure out that we were in here and . . ."

Price cut in, "It's not going to take them another ten bloody minutes if we don't get *out* of here, Yank! I wish you'd make up your mind and stick to one flaming plan at a time! I left the bloody timing devices down there in the bloody car!"

"You just keep working and I'll drop down and get them," said Evans, moving over to the ladder and starting down before the Welshman could argue. Price was all right. He just liked to bitch while he worked.

Evans just reached the next level of the cracking tower when a man in white coveralls came around the curve of the tower and called out, "Was machen Sie hier, mein Herr?"

Not speaking German, Evans smiled pleasantly at the technician, got within range, and threw a left hook. The German staggered back under the blow and grabbed the rail with both hands, shouting something that sounded like a cry for help.

Evans rabbit-punched him across the back of the neck, grabbed him by the seat of the pants, and heaved. The German screamed loudly, all the way down, until he hit with a loud, soggy thump.

Evans looked down at the still form at the bottom of the tower and scanned the surrounding area for any sign of activity. He saw Muller running over to the fallen man and went back to the ladder. Price called down, "What happened?" and Evans shouted "Keep working. I'll be with you in a minute!"

He got to the ground as Muller was dragging the dead

German toward the car. Muller smiled wanly and said, "We're running out of room in the trunk, sir."

Evans didn't look at the man he'd killed as he ran to the car, rummaged in the back seat for a set of timing devices, and trotted back to the ladder.

Muller called to Krinke, "Help me with this one, will you? He feels like a barracks bag full of Jello, and I'm getting crud all over my snazzy Nazi boots!"

ooo

The technician from the office turned to the sergeant of the guard and said, "That's odd. I don't see Gottlieb or the major anywhere. I was sure this was where we'd find them."

They were standing in the alleyway between the coal retorts and the catalytic chamber. The sergeant looked up at the jungle of pipes and catwalks and said, "I shouldn't have left my bike at the office. A man could get lost in all this plumbing."

The technician pointed to the cinder-covered earth and said, "Those are fresh tire tracks. They must have just driven off."

"Where do you suggest we look next?" asked the sergeant.

The technician shrugged and said, "I don't know. If his visit has something to do with those laborers from the concentration camp, they might have gone over to the coal tipples, near the canal." He pointed with his chin and added, "It's about a quarter kilometer from here. Do you

147

want to go back and get your bike?"

The sergeant said, "No. It's not that far, and I don't want to miss him before he leaves. Just point me in the right direction and I'll find him."

"Go to the next service road and turn toward the canal. You can't miss it. The coal tipples are near the cracking towers and you can see *them* from anywhere in the valley."

οοοοοοοοοοοοοοοοοοοοοοοοοοοοοοοοοοοοοοοοοοοοοοοοοο

In London, an American soldier with a Slavic sur-
name lay staring at the cracked ceiling over the bed and
wished he was a million miles away. The dumpy redhead
at his side ran a hand over his damp flesh and murmured,
"Oh, that was lovely. I want to do it again!"

The Communist spy said, "Let me get my breath back,
sweetheart," and wondered if he could get it up again. The
stupid slut had rotten teeth and her breath smelled like a
dog's. A man could overlook such imperfections in a
reasonably attractive woman. A man could even close his
eyes and pretend a dumpy potato-featured pig was pretty,
if she knew, at least, how to fuck.

But this one was a total disaster. She not only moved
badly, making those silly schoolgirl noises, but she had a
sloppy vagina big enough to service a horse. From the way
she acted, she'd probably screw a horse, if she could get
one up the stairs to her bedroom! You'd think a terminal
nymphomaniac would at least know how to tighten up
her snatch and move it right!

He stared some more at the ceiling, wondering why it had cracked that way. The cracks formed an almost perfect outline of the state of Texas. He'd been very good at geography at school, and he certainly knew a map of Texas when he saw one. There was another pattern, next to Texas. But it didn't look like any place he'd ever seen on a map. Maybe it was a crocodile?

The German spy ran her fingers through the pubic hairs of the Russian spy and cooed, "Oh, the poor little peepee's all shriveled and soft. Does it want kittikins to give it a French lesson?"

The man repressed a shudder as the redhead started kissing her way down his body with that moronic mouth of hers. This was the hardest part of his mission. He'd already *told* the stupid little pig about Operation Octane. Now he had to keep her occupied for the rest of the afternoon and take her to dinner and a show. He knew she'd want more sex when he brought her home. But if he timed it right, he could keep her out until midnight. His superiors had stressed the importance of keeping her from sending her message before at least ten. What time was it now?

He raised his head as the redhead started sucking his flaccid penis. The clock on the table said a quarter to two, Greenwich. It would be an hour later in Berlin. If he could just last until ten or so. . . . He winced and gasped, "For God's sake, watch those *teeth!*"

The woman growled a teddy bear growl and mumbled, "I'm going to eat you all up! I want you to come in my mouth this time!"

The Russian spy let his head fall back on the pillow and muttered, "At least that's *some* improvement!" under his breath.

He wondered if Comrade Stalin imagined how many sacrifices had to be endured for the cause. The lonely boredom of a spy's life was bad enough. He could take that, and it was exciting to set a fire or waylay an enemy in an alleyway. But this, this was ridiculous! Where in the name of Marx had it said he had to lay an idiot who called herself kittikins?

The German spy was better with her mouth than she was with the yawning chasm between her fat thighs, and slowly, he felt himself beginning to respond. She took her lips from his glans and husked, "Would you like to stick it in my po-po, lovikins?"

He gagged and said, "I'd rather not. Just keep on doing it the French way. But watch those fucking *teeth!*"

She swiveled on the bed, placing a knee on either side of his head as she pleaded. "You do me too!" and the Russian spy was sure he was going to vomit. He stared up into the matt of red hair above his face, thought about crab lice, and said, "I'm too hot to go sixty-nine. I want to come in your ass!"

"You're such a brute!" she purred, moving her pelvis away from his face, as she added, "I love it when you brutalize me!"

She got on her hands and knees near the foot of the bed, as the Russian spy swung his feet to the floor and stood up. He placed a hand on each fat buttock and she reached between her thighs to guide him into her upthrust rectum. She was dry down there and he had to thrust hard to force his way in. She moaned and said, "Oh, my God. It's so big! I want it all. I want you to *hurt* me with *all* of it, lovikins!"

The tired man thrust savagely, and it wasn't bad this way. He couldn't *hit* the stupid slut. But it gave him a certain pleasure to hurt her. He dug his nails into her soft backside and glanced at the clock. The minute hand had hardly moved, and he wondered what she'd say if he had a cigarette while he was pumping away like this. He supposed that would be asking for trouble. It was important to keep her away from her secret wireless set and . . .

"Come!" she commanded. "Let me feel you coming in my bowels!"

He lied, "I'm almost there," and started pumping harder. It was no use, he knew. But he'd count to fifty and fake it. What was she doing *now*, for God's sake? Oh, she was masturbating, eh? She took it this way like one of those prison queens he'd used that year he'd spent in jail. The memory excited him, and he started moving faster. But he decided to fake the orgasm and save a real one for later. He had to keep her busy for, dear God, another six or seven fucking *hours!*

○○○

Price and Evans reached the ground and headed for the car. The last decoy charge was in place, and it was time to start thinking of their own necks again.

Evans said, "Home, James!" and Krinke said, "Yes, *sir!*" and threw the staff car in gear. As they pulled away from the base of the cracking tower, a man in a blue gray uniform waved at them and shouted something. Evans said, "Keep driving. Head for the gate as if we didn't see him!"

Behind them, the Luftwaffe sergeant frowned and muttered aloud, "That wasn't Major Unger! What's going *on* around here?"

The car vanished around a turn, and the sergeant broke into a dog trot back the way he'd come. He had to get to a phone. He wasn't sure just what this was all about. But he had to report it to the lieutenant. The SS owed at least an explanation for all this nonsense!

Meanwhile, the staff car rolled toward the gate, and Krinke honked the horn imperiously. The guards on duty were the same ones as before, and this time, Farmer Dorfler didn't want another argument. He slid the gate wide and saluted as the car rolled through. Corporal Muller repressed a smile as he returned the salute. When they were out on the road, Krinke floored the gas pedal.

Evans snapped, "Slow down! We don't want to wind up in a ditch *now!* Just tool along and try not to attract attention!"

Muller chortled, "We did it! We drove right in and out like big-ass birds and the fucking Nazis never suspected a thing!"

Price grunted, "We're not out of the soup yet, lads. We're still in the flaming middle of Germany. We'd best start making tracks as soon as we get back to the others!"

Evans shook his head and said, "We lay low until after dark."

"Garn! every flaming minute we delay gives the perishing Nazis more time to get on to us! Moving through the woods in daylight may be risky. But they haven't started searching for those bloody SS men yet. I'd rather get a good head start before they start into the woods with dogs and torches!"

"Take it easy. We'll be on our way before they start looking for Unger and the others. Besides, we have to time it right. I can't radio our people in Zurich we're coming for a few hours yet. I don't want to risk a forced march into a fire fight with the Swiss border guards!"

Muller turned in his seat to ask, "Is that where we're going, captain? I didn't know the Swiss were on our side!"

"They're not on anybody's side," said Evans. "That's why I have to contact our agents in Zurich before we reach the frontier. They're meeting us at the border. They'll radio when the coast is clear to cross."

Muller grinned and said, "I get it, sir. We meet these American agents, and they get us to a plane or something, right?"

Price snorted and started to say something. But Evans nudged him and said, "They'll get us to a safe place, Muller. You just let me worry about the details."

Price asked, "What's the pass and countersign? That muck about Snow White and the Seven Dwarfs I heard you and our MI5 chaps talking over in Norwich?"

Evans sighed and said, "Thanks. I really wanted the pass and countersign given away! I don't want either of you men to say a word about what you just heard. That's a direct order. Any question about that?"

Muller frowned and asked, "Do you mean none of the guys are supposed to know their own password, sir?"

"I mean a secret's not a secret if twenty-two people *know* it, Muller! We're a night's march from the Swiss border, and should one of the men get separated from us, knowing the pass and countersign, we'd be in a hell of a mess. We wouldn't dare to use the code, knowing the Nazis might have it, and *without* the code, we just can't get out of Germany!"

"I see what you mean, sir," said Corporal Muller.

ooo

At the Kellermann farm, Sister Alfrieda was blushing as she stood in the bedroom doorway, explaining to Sergeant Compton that she had to attend a call to nature. Compton nodded and said, "You want to use the latrine? It's in the cellar, miss. I'll have one of the guys take you down."

He turned to the guards at the head of the stairs and called out, "Rogers, show the lady to the slit trench in the cellar and stay with her 'til she's done."

Trooper Rogers grinned and asked, "You mean I get to watch her take a crap?"

Compton said, "Knock it off. Can't you see she's red as a beet. Just run her down to the cellar and keep an eye on the door 'til she's through."

Rogers nodded and said, "Let's go, miss. I was only kidding."

The SS driver, Holzheim, came to the door of the room he and the farmer were confined to and said something in German. He was wearing one of the farmer's robes, a couple of sizes too big for him, and Compton smiled as he

156

asked the nurse, "What's *his* problem, miss?"

The nurse spoke to Holzheim in German for a time, and then she said in English, "He also must the latrine use."

"All that conversation just to go to the john?" said the sergeant. The girl sighed and said, "He also complaining he is wanting some . . . *hosen?* Ah, *pants* to put on."

Compton laughed and said, "Tell him he gets his uniform back when the captain's good and ready!"

The woman spoke to the driver in German. Major Unger came to the door of *his* room and got into the act with a long-winded comment of his own. Compton frowned and waved the muzzle of his carbine, saying, "All right, let's knock it off. The captain said I wasn't to let you people talk to one another in German until Krinke gets back!"

The nurse nodded and said, "Please, poor Holzheim English does not speak."

Compton shrugged and said, "That's *his* problem. If you want to use the latrine, go ahead. I don't see any reason to make a speech about it!"

Rogers said, "Come on, I'll take the driver down after you've finished in the cellar, fraw-lion."

Both of the male prisoners remained in the doorways as Rogers escorted the nurse downstairs. Major Unger said something to his driver and Compton snapped, "Get back in those fucking rooms. Both of you!"

Unger smiled and said, "That is what I just told him, Sergeant Compton," and stepped back out of sight. The driver went back to protest about something to the unseen farmer, and mollified, the sergeant walked to the stairs to join the one man still posted there. He said, "I wish the fucking captain would make up his mind. First he puts Krinke in charge of these Krauts and then he takes Krinke *off* someplace."

The trooper lounging at the head of the stairs asked,

"What's the difference? Those Krauts can't do anything in their fucking underwear."

"Did Conti's guys take over in the barn all right?"

"Sure. Smitty and Dunvegan are taking a break before they join Conti on perimeter guard. This sure is a boring mission, considering."

"That's the way I like my wars. I read someplace that wars are nine-tenths boredom and one-tenth sheer terror. You're not supposed to *enjoy* yourself *either* way."

"Hurry up and wait," agreed the trooper. "You know it's been like that since the day I joined up? If they're not running my ass off, I'm sitting around doing nothing. I mean, I transferred to the airborne because I thought it would be exciting, and here I am on a fucking combat mission, wasting a whole day doing nothing!"

Down in the cellar, Sister Alfrieda grimaced in distaste as she urinated in a corner, squatting over the evil-smelling slit trench. The farmer's wife had neglected to cover her droppings when she'd used the improvised latrine, and a blue-bottle fly was buzzing around the nurse's head as she stood up and kicked some loose dirt into the pit. The peasant woman upstairs was a filthy ignorant thing. But this was her cellar, and if she'd remembered correctly, her slovenly housekeeping might yet prove a service to the Third Reich.

Sister Alfrieda went across the dirt floor to a row of jarred preserves, racked on pine shelves against the dark north wall. She started removing the dusty jars, placing them quietly on the earth and searching the cobwebbed surface behind the dusty jars until her fingers touched a varnished wooden handle. She smiled in the gloom of the cellar and drew the ice pick from its hiding place. The farmer's wife had remembered leaving it here to pry wax plugs from her candied strawberries when opening a jar. God be thanked the woman had remembered where she'd left it, and that Ami hadn't found it!

She put the jars back, slipped the ice pick up her sleeve, and went up the cellar stairs to the kitchen. She lowered her eyes and pictured herself naked and masturbating in front of all the enemy soldiers in the room. It made her blush slightly, and one of the soldiers smirked. That was good. It was important they dismiss her as a shy young thing. The one called Rogers said, "Let's get you back upstairs and I'll run that other guy down to the latrine."

Sister Alfrieda called out to Holzheim when she reached the landing. The surly SS driver came to the door and spoke in German. Sister Alfrieda told the three Americans, standing there, "Please, he says he does not have to do it now."

Compton nodded and said, "Okay. You'd better go back to your room, miss."

Sister Alfrieda lowered her voice and murmured, "May I speak alone with you, sergeant? There is something you should know about those men I came here with."

Compton frowned and followed her into the bedroom. Frau Kellermann looked up from where she sat on the bed and Sister Alfrieda asked Compton, "Dare I ask the old woman to leave us alone? She may a little English understand, and this thing I have to tell you is not meant for German ears!"

Compton frowned and said, "Tell her to step outside. What's this all about, miss?"

Sister Alfrieda spoke to the farmer's wife in German, and the woman got up and went to stand outside in the hall as the sergeant called out, "It's okay. We're having a private conversation in here."

Rogers laughed, "Dibs on sloppy seconds, sarge!"

Compton smiled and turned to the nurse, his carbine slung muzzle down on his right shoulder, the hand resting on the banana clip.

Sister Alfrieda licked her lips, and the fright in her eyes was genuine as she said, "You must get word to the outside world about what is going on in these concentration camps! I came here to buy food for my children. But there is never enough. The party refuses to send the food and medical supplies I ask for."

"You mean those kids are starving over there? They told us Vogelbach was better than most concentration camps."

She stepped closer and said, "Not so *loud,* I beg you! If the major suspected I was telling you this, my life would not be worth as much to him as one of his Jews! You have heard, out in the real world, of the Final Solution?"

"No. What's the Final Solution?"

"They are going to kill them all. All of the Jews. All of the Gypsies. All of the Slavs. All of the people they are holding in these many camps! You must get word to the International Red Cross. They have to know what men like Konrad Unger are really like!"

She put her left hand out, taking the lapel of Compton's jump suit between her trembling fingers, and whispered, "Take me with you when you leave! I cannot stand the things they make me do! I am a nurse. My whole life has been dedicated to helping people. I must myself to the Red Cross speak and tell them what the Nazis are really like!"

Compton said, "I don't know, miss. I can ask the captain, when he gets back. But I don't think . . ."

"You must!" she sobbed, clutching at the lapel and swaying weakly. Compton put out a hand to steady her, saying, "Hey, take it easy, honey!" as she let the ice pick slide from its hiding place, caught it by the handle, and moved with the speed and skill that had made her champion of the women's team at the Strength through Joy Lager. The sergeant stiffened at the sudden movement. But her aim was true as she brought the ice pick up and drove it to the hilt in his left nostril. She twisted it, whirling the steel tip around inside his brain as she held him erect by the firm grip on his lapel. The man's knees buckled, and she let go of the ice pick to heave him on the bed with both strong arms. Her heart was beating wildly, but her hands were the firm hands of a true Nordiche Walkure as she slipped the slung carbine free of the twitching corpse and snicked the safety off.

She stepped to the doorway, shouted, "Los! Heraus!" and fired, full automatic, into the three people at the head of the stairs.

Major Unger and the other SS man dashed out of their rooms as the German farm woman and the two paratroopers went down. The major ran to the nearest dead American, scooped up his fallen carbine, and started down, three steps at a time. Behind him, Holzheim hesitated only long enough to arm himself, and with the deadly blonde bringing up the rear, all three erupted into the kitchen, shooting from their hips.

Two more troopers went down before they knew what hit them. The Russian called Boris dove head first out the kitchen door as his companion stood rooted in terror by the hot stove. A carbine round took him just over the belt buckle, and he fell against the hot metal, screaming. Major Unger jumped over a dying paratrooper and ran outside, just as his purloined staff car skidded to a stop in the farmyard!

Unger hosed the car with automatic fire as Corporal Muller jumped out, raising his German pistol. Muller fired as two rounds snuffed his heart out. His one shot missed Unger but hit the SS man behind him in the chest. Holzheim staggered and kept on coming, his own stolen carbine chattering like a mad woodpecker as the nurse came out, firing cool short bursts and taking aim.

Across the farmyard, a pair of carbines spoke as one, and the major fell to his knees, snarling in rage and pain as he emptied the clip in his weapon at the men diving out the far side of the staff car. Sister Alfrieda cursed and swung the muzzle of her own weapon up to fire into the hay loft. A man from Sergeant Conti's stick came running around the corner of the house, took the whole scene in at a glance, and shot Sister Alfrieda twice in the body and once in the head before she dropped, still shooting. He put another burst into Holzheim as the Nazi dropped his weapon and started to raise his hands. Holzheim staggered back, tripped over Sister Alfrieda's body, and fell spread-eagled on his back. A final shot from the barn took the top off Major Unger's skull, and then it got very quiet for a moment.

Somewhere in the house, a husky voice was sobbing, "Momma! Offne Deine Augen, Momma!" and Krinke got up from behind the car, muttering, "Jesus Christ!"

Near the rear bumper, Matt Price shook the captain's shoulder and said, "All clear, mate. Are you all right?"

Evans didn't answer. Price rolled him half over, saw what a bullet had done to the captain's right eye, and let go of the body, sighing, "Coo! They fixed *your* flaming wagon, didn't they, Yank?"

Krinke turned and gasped, "Jesus, is the captain wounded?"

Price said, "No. He's dead. You'd best get Sergeant Conti. Tell him he's in command now and ask him what in bloody hell he wants to do about it!"

○○

In London, a church bell tolled six times, and a Soviet agent opened his eyes to wonder where he was. He stared up at the map of Texas on the ceiling, reached lazily out to caress the woman at his side, and muttered. "I must have dozed off. Was that six I just heard?"

His body stiffened and he came full awake as he realized he was alone in the bed! He sat up, swung his feet to the floor, and staggered to the clothes he'd left on the chair, cursing himself for a fool. What could have possessed him to let his guard fall like that? How long had he been asleep? It was too early for that red-headed slut to contact OKW! He had to stop her!

He drew a small Browning automatic from its secret pocket in his American jacket and, still naked, tiptoed out into the hall. He started up to the attic, moving on the balls of his bare feet until he reached a door at the top. He placed a hand on the knob and gently twisted. The goddamned door was locked on the other side!

He braced to smash it open with his shoulder. Then he

heard the woman's voice through the thin panels and sucked his breath in sheer panic. It was too late. She was on the wireless in there, and there was no telling how much she'd already told them! How in God's name was he going to explain this to his superiors?"

He considered killing her. Killing her would give him at least a chance to get a running start. But where was he supposed to run to? If he went AWOL from the damned American army, he'd have *them* after him too! The only people he could go to, in England, were his fellow Communists. But he couldn't go to *them*. Not *now!* He'd just made a terrible blunder, and he knew no explanation he could give would keep them from the punishment he deserved for letting the damned Nazis steal a march on him!

He swiftly slipped back down to the bedroom, threw on his clothes, and tucked his weapon away for the moment. He had to get out of here fast and do some serious thinking!

He left the house before the woman finished her transmission. He started walking, not yet sure just where he wanted to go. He *might* be able to convince them he'd kept her from sending the message until midnight. But they had agents everywhere. What if someone in Berlin told Comrade Petrovich when the Nazis got the word? He knew they wouldn't tell *him*. They'd follow the usual procedure, telling him he'd done well, until they could arrange for his liquidation. Hadn't *he* taken care of untrustworthy comrades that way often enough?

A cab was coming down the block. The Communist agent hailed it and got in. The driver turned and asked, "Where to, sir?" and the Communist spy sighed, "Take me to the American Embassy."

∘∘

Pete Conti watched Gilmore and Blanchard smoothing down the dirt over the mass grave in the barn as Price was saying, "Be dark in a bit, sergeant. What do you say we get a move on?"

Conti said, "Shut up, I'm thinking!" and went on counting on his fingers. The captain, Compton, Corporal Muller, and six troopers were dead, if you counted Murphy, who wasn't going to last much longer with those three rounds in his gut. That left a dozen asses he had to worry about, besides his own. The one Russian left had said he could get home with a passport from one of the two dead Germans they'd brought back in the trunk. That left the old man. What was he supposed to do with the old man?

Aloud, he said, "I guess we'll have to tie the farmer up or something."

Price said flatly, "You have to kill him. There's no other way. Krinke can do it. It's a waste of time to have him watching the old beggar, and Kellermann's half out of his mind with grief over his wife. You saw how mad those other Jerries acted, and there's no telling what the old man will try. I say kill him!"

"You want the job?" asked Conti.

Price looked away and said, "Garn, I'm only a perishing technician!"

"Well, then, shut up about it, if you haven't got the balls to do it yourself. Right now, I've got to figure out our best way out of here. You say Snow White's the pass and one of the Seven Dwarfs is supposed to answer?"

"Not just any dwarf, sarge. As I understand it, Grumpy means the coast is clear, Sneezy is the signal to lay low, and Dopey means they can't talk and you're to call back in an hour."

Conti nodded and said, "Let's go back to the house and see if I can reach them on the R-300, then."

Price followed him out of the barn, saying, "Evans said he wasn't supposed to call before he was within a few miles of the Swiss frontier, sarge."

Conti said, "I don't give a shit *what* the captain said. He *lied* to us, Price! Nobody ever said anything about us surrendering to anybody before they sent us on this fucking mission!"

"I know. But now you have no choice. The thirteen of us can hardly afford to take on the whole flaming German army!"

Conti entered the house, shot a look at the kitchen floor, and told the nearest trooper, "Get a mop bucket and GI this fucking floor. There's blood and crud all over it!"

The trooper said, "Shit, sarge, it's not as if we figured to *be* here all that long."

But Conti snapped, *"Do* it, soldier!" and went on into the front parlor. He found the R-300 pack on a table and trooper Murphy laying on a couch with another man bending over him. Conti asked, "How's it going, Murph?"

The wounded man groaned, "Not so hot. Can I have

something to drink, sarge? I'm thirsty as hell!"

Conti said, "Not with abdominal wounds, Murph."

"What's the difference? I'm dying anyway, ain't I?"

Conti smiled and said, "Not without a direct order. You just lay still and hang in there, soldier. I gotta talk to a dwarf."

He went to the table, flicked on the battery-operated radio pack, and took a seat at the table. He waited until the tubes warmed up and picked up the headset, feeling foolish as he sent, "Snow White calling, uh, CQ. Repeat. Snow White calling CQ. Come in CQ. Over."

He listened to the headset, hearing a far-away sound of music. He adjusted the tuning until there was only white noise and repeated the passwords, over and over. There was no answer and he looked up at Price to ask, "Are you sure I'm on the right frequency?"

"The captain had the dials set. See those white marks he made?"

Conti nodded and repeated the call. After a while, he heard a far-away voice saying something in German and told Price, "Get Krinke. The Seven Dwarfs are out digging diamonds or something. All I'm picking up is Kraut."

○○○

The Eighth Air Force had been over Berlin that after-noon and the telephone lines were a mess. But the call was routed through from Kassel, and a phone rang in the OKW bunker. A tried officer picked it up and said, "Here speaks Von Dreihausen."

The voice at the other end was blurred and excited as it said, "We just received word from London, Herr Oberst! That Anglo-American mission was aimed at the hydro-genation works at Vogelbach!"

Von Dreihausen said, "I'll call at once and have them double the guard tonight. It's nearly dark out, and Ami won't move until then. Have you verified the report?"

"An agent in London got it from an American soldier she's been sleeping with. She called in less than an hour ago with the whole story!"

The OKW man got up with the phone in his hand to look at the wall map. He frowned and said, "I think the story sounds a little crazy. Why would they send in a sui-cide mission when they have air superiority in that sector?

Why not simply bomb the place from the air? Who *is* this agent who spends so much of her time in bed with Americans?"

"Mary Magdalene is her code name, Herr Oberst."

Von Dreihausen snorted and said, "You waste my time with a report from *her?* Don't you know the other side knows about that hyperkinetic redhead? Agent Mary Magdalene is a dirty joke, damn it!"

"Herr Oberst, I'm afraid I do not understand!"

"What is there to understand? Allied intelliegnce has their men taking turns sleeping with the poor slut! I understand they have to offer a three-day pass as compensation."

"You mean they *know* she works for us, Herr Oberst? Why haven't they *arrested* her?"

"I'll be damned if I know. They tell me she's not worth going to bed with. But they keep doing it anyway, and feeding her such misinformation as she just transmitted."

"Ach! I see it all now. The story about Vogelbach is a ruse, to keep us from finding out the *real* mission!"

"Why, no, they *always* send us word of what their plans are. I'd better contact the SS at Vogelbach, just in case. But I'm sure it's a false alarm."

"Why call at all, Herr Oberst?"

"Because we can't afford to take chances in this business, and anyway, it won't hurt those lazy dogs to prowl about in the woods one night."

oo

Corporal Krinke handed the headset back to Sergeant Conti and said, "It's something about an air raid on Berlin, sarge. We're picking them up, on the edge of this wave band. But I don't think they can hear us. It's a loose tube or something in our receiver."

Conti swore and said, "Keep calling CQ as Snow White, then. How's Gilmore getting along with that Kraut upstairs?"

Krinke shrugged and answered, "Kellermann doesn't speak English, and Gilmore doesn't know a word of German. But what can you say, in any language, to a guy who's just seen his wife shot dead before his eyes? He kept asking me, before, how come the *Germans* shot his wife. But I couldn't answer any better than Gilmore."

Conti stepped over by the couch, looked down at Murphy, and didn't say anything. Then, as Krinke started calling CQ on the R-300, the sergeant spread the air force map on the floor and squatted over it on his haunches.

The Air Force map was printed on silk and made a

dandy scarf or bandana. Since thousands of flyboys had given them away to girls, this particular map had been recoded in indelible laundry marker by the late Captain Evans. Conti hadn't been consulted on the matter. But it was easy enough to see how it worked. The numbered coordinates around the borders of the map had been changed to a random sequence of new figures. The Seven Dwarfs would have a duplicate, coordinated the same way. Evans had drawn a zigzag route from the DZ, here, to a stretch along the Swiss frontier. It was a detailed contour map and the planned route seemed to be a good one, following the ridges and avoiding roads and settled areas. Conti studied the map carefully, running his eyes over each square in detail before moving to the next. After a time he stabbed a finger down on the soft silk and asked Krinke, "What's a *Horst?*"

"Depends on how it's used," answered the corporal. "Could be a bird's nest, or a flat-topped mountain."

Conti nodded and said, "I'm betting on the last meaning. The contour lines show a wide, flat ridge about, uh, twenty miles from here as the crow flies. We won't be riding no crow. So let's say it's more like thirty with the zigs and zags. Take us, oh, less than ten hours, give or take a fire fight along the way."

He looked at his watch and added, "It's quarter to eight. Be dark enough to move in half an hour. Say we roll out at eight-thirty . . . We'd be there just about dawn. That's cutting it pretty close. But there don't seem to be any buildings along that, uh, Horst. The map shows woods all around it."

Krinke said, "Snow White calling CQ. Come in, CQ. Over." Then he asked the sergeant, "Where is it, sarge? Between here and the Swiss border?"

Conti said, "Not exactly. It's sort of north-northeast of here."

Krinke frowned and said, "North-northeast? That's

taking us right in the direction of *Berlin,* for Christ's sake!"

Conti shrugged and said, "Can't be helped. It's the only flat country I can find that hasn't got a Kraut town plastered all over it!"

He got to his feet, went into the kitchen, and inspected the freshly mopped floor. A trooper was seated at the kitchen table, drinking a mug of coffee. Conti frowned down at him and asked, "Have you guys finished putting this place back together?"

The trooper said, "We even made the fucking beds, sarge. Who's going to pull this inspection you're getting ready for, General Eisenhower?"

"Get out to the yard and police it for brass and butts."

"We did already. There's not a cartridge case or Chesterfield butt for miles, sarge. We've done everything but whitewash the rocks!"

Conti frowned at the fresh wood splinters where a bullet had torn a divot from the jamb of the kitchen door and said, "That's not a bad idea. Get some of that paint we mixed up to disguise the car and mix it with some dirt. I want as many bullet holes as you can see in this light puttied over before we leave. We're leaving in less than an hour. So get the lead out."

The trooper stood up, saying, "You sure are leaving this place in good shape, sarge. Is there any particular reason, or do you just like to keep the troops busy?"

Conti said, "The Krauts will be sniffing around here sooner or later. I don't want to leave them any messages we've been here."

"Come on, sarge. They'll find the blood and bullet holes, once they start looking!"

"So let's make them *look,* damn it! I want the cups and saucers piled in the sink too. Put a full charge of wood in the stove and make sure it's going when we pull out. I want it to look like the farmer and his wife just went down the road for a game of Monopoly or something at another farm."

"What are we gonna do with Murphy and the old man, sarge? Won't the Krauts find *them* sooner or later?"

"I'd rather make it later than sooner. You just police the area and let me figure out what we do with Murph and the old man."

He went back in the parlor and stared morosely down at the dying trooper. Murphy sensed his presence and opened his eyes. Conti smiled and said, "You're doing fine, Murph. Just hang on for an hour or so and you'll be in like Flynn!"

Murphy licked his dry lips and asked, "Who are we kidding, Pete? I should have been dead an hour ago."

"Hey, Murph, come on, you never had it so good!"

"You don't have to bullshit me, Pete. I've had time to get used to the idea, and you know what? I'm not scared. I'm not scared at all. I was sort of scared and surprised at first. But it's all right now. I'm not going to crybaby it. You'll see."

Conti nodded and said, "I know that, Murph. But let's not play hero either, huh? We've still got plenty of morphine, if you need it. You start to hurt again, you give a holler. Hear?"

Murphy managed a slight nod and said, "Before you bury me, I got some junk in my pockets. You'll see the folks get it, huh?"

Conti nodded but said, "Nobody's going to bury anybody, Murph. I'm taking you with me either way."

Across the room, Krinke suddenly gasped, "Sarge! I got a dwarf!"

Conti moved swiftly to grab the headset from him. He clapped the receiver against his ear in time to hear, "This is Bashful, Snow White. You've called too early. Move to map coordinates V-23 by H-48 and await further instructions. Over."

Conti flicked the sending switch and said, "Negative, Bashful. We're meeting you at V-129 by H-163. We'll need transport for fourteen. One of us will be on a litter. Over."

There was a long silence at the other end, and Conti thought, for a time, they'd broken off contact. Then another voice came on to say, "Negative, Snow White! That was not the plan. We have no way of getting to you at that location. Proceed to V-23 by H-48 and stick to the original plan! Over!"

Conti smiled thinly and said, "I don't know the original plan. They *shot* the motherfucker who kept all those cute ideas to himself! As the ranking NCO, I'm taking my people out the best way I know how. We'll need roughly ten hours to reach V-129 by H-163. So that gives you a whole night to work something out. Over."

The agent in Zurich snapped, "Goddamn it, Snow White, I'm *ordering* you to meet us at V-23 by H-48! My rank is lieutenant colonel, in case you're in doubt about my authority. Over."

"I'm a tech sergeant," said Conti, "and I don't *give* a fuck who *you* are! I've got thirteen survivors here. One of them's hurt bad. I'm taking them where I said I was taking them, and you can either meet us or blow it out your ass! Over!"

"We can't possibly meet you at those coordinates, damn it! I repeat, Snow White, you have a direct order to carry out the original plan! Over!"

Conti said, "Negative. I read the book too. There's only one order any soldier in any army is free to disobey at his own discretion, and there's nothing in my discretion about *surrendering* to *anybody!* I'm taking my people to V-129 by H-163. You guys do what you like. Over."

There was another long silence. Then the agent in Zurich said, "Goddamn you, sergeant! I'm going to have you court-martialed for this! We *can't* meet you where you suggest! Over!"

Conti grinned and said, "If you want to court-martial me, you'll have to come and *get* me, *won't* you? Over."

"Listen, son, it can't be done! Not on such short notice! Why not head for the original coordinates while I get in touch with someone, eh? Over."

"Negative. We're going where I said we're going. Over."

"We're not meeting you there! You'll be cut off and captured, you idiot! There's no way out of that area on foot! Repeat no way! Over!"

Conti shrugged and said, "That's your problem. All I'm worried about, right now, is getting my people to where you can pick us up. Take another look and you'll see it's not that tough. I've got to sign off, colonel. We've both got a lot to do tonight. Over and out!"

The short colonel in Zurich said, "Wait! Let's talk this over, son!" But Conti switched the set off without answering. He smiled at Krinke and said, "Let's see if we can get Murph, here, to the car. I figure we can all pile on and drive a good five miles into the woods before we have to ditch it."

⦿⦿⦿

The Tall General was a study in controlled rage as he slammed down the phone, turned to his secretary, and snapped, "They just got a message from Zurich. I'm already late for a staff meeting, and those silly son's of bitches I sent to sabotage that hydrogenation plant at Vogelbach are headed in the wrong direction!"

The WAC asked, "Is Dave Evans all right?"

"Beats the shit out of me!" the general replied. "Zurich says they report heavy casualties. But MI5 says their field operators haven't picked up anything from the Germans. How in hell could they have lost so many men without the Germans knowing about it? There's got to be a screw loose somewhere!"

He looked at his watch, said, "Jesus, Bradley's going to have my ass if I miss another Overlord briefing! You'd better stay here and hold the fort tonight."

Then he scooped a briefcase up from his desk and went out the door, not answering as his secretary asked, "What are your orders on Operation Octane?"

She found herself alone and muttered, "Shit, there goes my date with that dreamy pilot!"

She opened a drawer, got out a coded map, and reached for a phone, asking the operator to put her through to OSS.

A man answered and she said, "I'm calling for the general about that snafu at Vogelbach. Is this Howie?"

The OSS man answered, "Barbara? Hey, how's it going, beautiful? Those guys you sent to knock that plant out are all turned around! They seem to be making a forced march on Berlin!"

"Is there no way to bail them out? What's the coordinates on the place they're going?"

"V-129 by H-163. It's a sort of mesa in the Bavarian National Forest Preserve. I don't know what the hell they expect to do when they *get* there. They were supposed to be going the other way!"

The WAC found the position on her map and said, "It looks as if they expect to be picked up. One plane could lift out fourteen men, couldn't it?"

"We've been around that block with Air Operations. The ridge is too short for a Mosquito to land and take off."

"What about a C-47? I understand *those* kites can land on a ping-pong table, if they have to."

"Negative on a C-47, Barbara. Those big kites are too slow for a mission like you're suggesting. Night fighter catches all that aluminum on its radar and it's all over. Goddamn C-47 can't fight and it can't run. Besides, the jerks are disobeying orders. It's their own damned fault if the Krauts nail them!"

The WAC sighed and said, "I guess you're right." She remembered Dave Evans and how nice he was in bed. They'd made a date to meet again sometime, and letting the Germans have him seemed such a waste.

Another phone was ringing, and she said, "I'll get back to you, Howie," and hung up. She picked up the second phone and heard, "This is Flannery, CIC. I've just been talking to a mechanic from the 448th Bomb Group who turned himself in at the embassy tonight."

The WAC frowned and said, "Wait a minute. You say an *American* GI just turned himself in? For *what,* sweet Santa Maria?"

"The guy's a Soviet agent. He's asking for political asylum. Seems his conscience is bothering him, or he just blew a job for our Red buddies, or both."

"So what's his story?"

"He says he passed your Operation Octane on to a German spy in the West End. We picked her up an hour ago, and she's verified it. The Krauts know all about the mission. They'll be waiting for them as they move in!"

The WAC said, "Oh, boy! I'll get back to you later!"

She dialed SHAEF and asked for the general. She was told he wasn't there yet, and she asked them to have him call his office as soon as he arrived. Then she dialed OSS and said, "Howie, we're in trouble. OKW knows about the mission. We have to head them off at the pass!"

The OSS man answered, "I'll call Zurich and see what they know. I may be wrong. But I got the impression they've *finished* at the plant and want *out!* I'll see what MI5 has too and call you back."

Out in the night, an air-raid siren started to moan, and the WAC felt suddenly very lonely in the empty office. It was probably only another drill. The Luftwaffe hadn't been getting this far inland for some time. She'd wait until the ack-ack opened up before she went to the shelter. The general would have a fit if he called and found her gone with all this shit hitting the fan!

Seven blocks away, an air-raid warden waved a staff car over to the side and called, "Take shelter, mates. Nobody moves until the all clear sounds!"

The Tall General got out of the rear seat and said, "See

here, I'm due at an important meeting! You have to let us through!"

The warden shook his head and said, "I have my orders, sir."

"Oh, Hell, I'll walk!" the Tall General said. "I'm going to be late anyway. May as well have a good excuse!"

An SS officer picked up the phone and said, "Here speaks SS Zug Leutnant Pfalz, Lager Vogelbach," and a voice said, "Let me speak to Major Unger. I'm calling from OKW."

"The major is not here at the moment," Pfalz replied. He's, ah, out on an inspection."

It was the least he could do for a brother officer. But where in thunder *was* the skirt-chasing idiot?

The OKW man said, "I'm calling about a possible airborne attack in your area. We have a rumor that American paratroop commandos are about to pay you a visit!"

"Ami paratroopers, *here?*"

"They may be after the hydrogenation plant, actually. You'd better get some men over there to give the regular guard a hand. The sun's going down, and if there's anything to it, they'll be hitting any minute. You'd better get some counterpatrols out too. I'll call you back as soon as we have a better idea just how authentic the report was."

The lieutenant heard a click, frowned, and put down

the phone. He went to the door and shouted, "Feldwebel!"

His sergeant major jumped up from his own desk and snapped to attention as the lieutenant said, "Assemble the reserve guard. It looks like we're about to have a busy night!"

oo

Pete Conti walked around the car in the gloaming light and wondered what he was doing wrong. The dying Murphy had been placed in the trunk. Gilmore and another trooper were wedged in with him, their feet on the rear bumper and their shoulders holding the lid open. Price and the farmer were up front with Krinke behind the wheel. Another four were piled in the back with the radio pack. That left five places on the running boards and four troopers had already climbed aboard. Conti went to the driver's window, got on the running board, and said, "Let's go, Krinke. Across the field and up that fire road I showed you on the map."

Krinke started the engine, saying, "It's getting pretty dark, sarge. Do we use the headlights?"

Conti said, "No. I can see pretty good out here. Drive slow and I'll tell you if we're coming to a low bridge. But let's move it, shall we?"

The car lurched forward, amid a chorus of laughter and curses. It was down on its shocks under the heavy load, and something snapped as the rear wheels bounced over the shallow ditch between Kellermann's farmyard and the meadow beyond. Krinke gave it more gas and the car kept rolling. Mercedes made a pretty good automobile, thought Krinke. He hadn't expected it to start after taking all those bullets through the hood back there.

They got three quarters of the way to the other side of the meadow before Conti punched Krinke's shoulder and said, "Kill the engine! Now!"

Krinke switched off the ignition without waiting for further explanations as Conti dropped from the running board and hissed, "Everybody off and down! Somebody just pulled into the farm back there!"

Krinke started to open the door on his side. But Conti snapped, *"Quiet,* goddamn you! Just sit tight and try not to breathe! I don't think they can see us from the house!"

Conti eased away from the car, holding his carbine at port, as he studied the moving flashes of light around the black hulk of the farmhouse and outbuildings. He never should have let that damned Russian take off like that. The cocksucker's done right to the nearest phone and called the fucking Nazis!

Inside the car, Kellermann suddenly shoved at Price and tried to shout as the Welshman clapped a hand over his mouth. Price hissed, "Don't bite, you bloody sod! Somebody help me, for God's sake!"

A trooper in the rear seat reached forward, grabbed the farmer by the hair and yanked his head back savagely as Krinke reached for the knife in his jump boot. The farmer was stronger than Price and managed to twist his face away from the Welshman's palm long enough to shout, "Helfe!" in a husky voice.

Then Price clapped a bleeding palm to his lips, even as Krinke backhanded the knife into the farmer's twisting body, catching him under a floating rib and twisting the handle down hard, to reach the wildly beating heart with the point.

The German stiffened, farted, and went limp as Conti ran over to hiss, "Keep him *quiet* in there!"

Krinke swallowed the green taste in his mouth and said, "We just did," and pulled the knife out. He wiped the blade on the farmer's pants as Price observed, "He shit his breeches too. We'd better roll him out of here before we get it all over us!"

Conti said, "Hold it! We have to take him at least a few miles before we dump him. Just brace him up some way and keep it down to a roar. I've got to watch the fucking house!"

Six hundred yards away, an SS man came out of the kitchen door to shout, "There's nobody upstairs, Herr Leutnant!"

The patrol leader turned to one of the troopers in the yard to ask, "Anything in the barn, Heger?"

"No, Herr Leutnant. Not even the cows. They must be out there in the meadow."

The officer nodded and said, "I think I just heard one. The old man and his wife can't be planning to be away too long, if they haven't bedded the livestock down for the night."

He turned the beam of his flashlight toward the meadow, sweeping across the grass absently, as he mused, "We'll drop by again on our return sweep. I was sure the major said something about stopping here today for a side of veal."

One of his men chuckled and said, "If I know anything about the old man, he's probably spending the night with that Sister Alfrieda. You know what they say about *her*, Herr Leutnant."

The officer snapped, "That's enough of that kind of talk, damn it! I won't have any of you men showing disrespect to officers of the Reich!"

He flashed the light on his wrist and muttered, under his breath, "It's probably true. But such talk is dangerous." In a louder tone, he said, "Los, we're not going to find any Ami paratroopers around *here*. Let's move on to the next farm!"

One of his men pointed directly at the spot where Conti and his men were sweating it out and said, "We can save a kilometer by cutting across the fields, Herr Leutnant!"

The officer considered. Then shook his head and said, "The evening mists are rolling in and that tall grass will be wet in a little while. We'll follow the road and get there with dry boots. I don't want to catch my death chasing imaginary paratroopers through the woods like elves!"

ooo

A British subject, living in Berlin under an assumed
name, placed a wire spool in a special apparatus, flicked
a switch, and ran his clandestine radio for less than three
full seconds. A burst of staccato noise flashed across the
airways of Occupied Europe and was picked up by a
complex radio receiver in England. Those few Germans
who might have heard the short tearing sound might well
have put it down to static. Had they known enough to
record it, the message was in code anyway.

At MI5 in London, a technician rerecorded the burst
at slow speed. Then he ran the resultant gibberish through
an electronic device to unscramble it. The final result was
what looked like a long length of ticker tape, reading,
"Z-64 AT OKW REPORTS ENEMY DUBIOUS
OPERATION OCTANE BUT TAKING USUAL SE-
CURITY MEASURES STOP. IF MISSION ACCOM-
PLISHED ENEMY KNOWS NOTHING ABOUT IT
STOP. CANNOT VERIFY SNOW WHITE'S CAS-
UALTY REPORT STOP. OKW HAS NO INFO RE

FIGHTING NEAR DZ STOP. SUGGEST LANDING INJURIES NOT FIRE FIGHT STOP. NEXT TRANSMISSION 0300 OVER AND OUT."

The MI5 man at the liaison desk studied the report and muttered "I wonder what those Yanks have gotten themselves into. How could they have taken nineteen or twenty casualties without the bloody Jerries knowing about it?"

The man at the next desk asked, "Do you suppose Jerry knows some things he's keeping to himself?"

"I don't see how. The operator we have at OKW has a tap on old Von Dreihausen's personal phones. If *any* of those mucking bastards know anything, Von Dreihausen does. I'd better get this to the Americans. They'll want to know about that other chap too."

"The FFI has what's-his-name, Yellowpony, tucked safely away for the night?"

"Yes. They did a lovely job, for Frogs. Snatched him right out of the hospital and left a dead Gestapo man in his place. De Gaulle's people will be pleased too. But of course, we can't tell *that* lot anything until it's all over. We've orders not to tell those prima donnas anything until they learn to keep away from newspaper reporters!"

He picked up a phone, dialed the Tall General's office number, and said, "Evening, Barbara. I thought I'd better bring you up to date on Operation Octane, as far as we can learn from here."

"What's going on?" asked the WAC at the other end. "All I know is that the situation's normal, all fucked up!"

The MI5 man grimaced and said, "The Jerries seem to be in the dark too. They're running about in total confusion over in Berlin. They know something's going on. But they haven't put it together yet. Where do we go from here?"

The WAC said, "It beats the shit out of me! I'm waiting for His Nibs to get back from SHAEF Maybe *he* can figure it out!"

©©©

Sergeant Conti said, "Stop the car!" and jumped off
the running board before Krinke braked to a full stop.
Conti ran to the watchtower at the end of the fire road,
slung his carbine, and climbed the ladder to the one-room
shed atop the four wooden stilts. The watchtower was
empty and he couldn't see much from up here in the
dark. He climbed back down as the others were sorting
themselves out around the car and said, "End of the line.
We have to leg it from here."

He walked around to the rear of the car and asked,
"How's old Murph, Gilmore?"

Gilmore said, "He died a while back, sarge. Started
puking blood all over me and there wasn't a thing I
could do."

Conti said, "Cut some saplings and rig up some way to
carry Murph and the Kraut. I've got to get on the R-300
again."

Gilmore asked, "Are we taking both of them *with* us,
sarge?"

Conti said, "Just Murph, if we can. I don't want them to find the farmer's body here with the car. We'll bury him a mile or so down the pike and give the Krauts some detective work. They'll see the bullet holes, think those SS jerks ran into something up *here* and . . . what the fuck, let them figure it out any way they like!"

He hauled the R-300 pack from the rear seat, balanced it on the running board, and switched it on. He waited for the tubes to warm, and this time, they were waiting to hear from him.

Bashful said, "Snow White, the Wicked Witch wants to know if you completed your homework. Over."

"Mission accomplished," Conti said. "Now get us out of here! Over!"

"What's your present position, Snow White? Over."

"About six, seven miles from the DZ. En route to V-129 by H-163. We'll be there about sunrise. Over."

The man in Zurich pleaded, "Goddamn it, Snow White, you're going the wrong way! We have no way, repeat, *no way* to meet you at that location! Follow the original plan. Repeat, follow the *original plan!* We've taken your suggestion under consideration and the flyboys say it's hopeless! Over!"

Conti said, "We'll meet you there around 0600. We'll signal with three smudge fires if it's safe to come down. Over and out."

Then he switched off the set and stood up, yawning. He was tired as hell. But it was too early to break out the benzedrine tablets. He'd wait until the guys were really bushed before he issued stimulants. He'd seen some guys act pretty wild on benzedrine and a cool, tired head beat a hopped-up head in any fight. He found Price by the front of the car and said, "Let's get the dead Kraut out and push this heap over the edge. Looks like a good steep incline past the tower."

Price asked, "Why not leave him in the car? And why

wreck it anyway? It won't take them all that longer to find it down in the ravine, you know."

Conti said, "If it takes them another ten minutes, it's worth *one* to roll it over the edge. They'll waste time looking for the passengers down in those bushes too."

Price said, "Let's get on with it, then." He reached in the car to drag the dead farmer out by the feet. The corpse's head thunked loudly on the running board and thudded to the dirt of the road. Price dragged the body clear and put a shoulder to the doorjamb, saying, "Over the side with the perishing thing and let's be off!"

Conti grabbed a doorpost and heaved. A couple of other men helped, and together, they ran the car to the end of the road and off the edge. It rolled down the steep incline with surprising sedateness, snapping saplings off but staying on all four wheels until it was out of sight. The sound of breaking branches continued for a time. Then faded to silence. Conti said, "Jesus, all my life I wanted to shove a car off a cliff, and when I got to do it . . ."

"It's hung up in the trees downslope," said Price.

Conti said, "All right. It's time to get moving. I'll call the guys together and . . ."

"Wait," said Price. "There's something I have to get right with you, sergeant."

"Make it fast, Mister Price. We have a long row to hoe before this night is over."

Price said, "I'm not going with you lot. I've done this sort of work before and I think I can make it on my own to Switzerland."

"Are you nuts, Price? You'd never make it alone, and if you did, the Swiss would put you in prison for the duration!"

"Not prison, mate. Just house arrest at a posh hotel. I can see *your* reasons for not wanting to be interned. But I'm in another boat, you see. I have blokes looking for me, to do me in. Blokes that can't get at me in Zurich. I can make it on my own. Ay, and cross the border too!"

Conti shook his head and said, "No deal. We've got to stick together, Mister Price."

"But what bloody difference can it make to you, mate? It's *my own* ruddy arse I'm risking, ain't it?"

"No. It's all our asses, if the Krauts pick you up before we reach our objective. We're all going there together, Mister Price. That's a direct order."

Price snorted and said, "What right have you to order me? I'm a British subject, in the first place, and I outrank you in the second. By rights, I could order you lot to follow me to Switzerland!"

"Try it," Conti said, "and after the guys get through laughing, I'll kick the shit out of you, myself!"

"Why, you bloody little pup! I've whipped the arses of men twice your flaming size!"

"So I'll have to fight dirty, Mister Price. And even if you whip me, you're *still* coming with me and the others! You're coming if I have to drag you by the fucking heels, and if I can't drag you, myself, I'll ask for help."

Corporal Krinke had come up during the exchange and his voice was carefully casual as he asked, "Somebody ask for help, sarge?"

Conti said, "I don't think so. We were just bullshitting. Isn't that right, Mister Price?"

Price shrugged and said, "If you say so, sergeant."

Conti nodded and said, "Right. Let's pick up the bodies and the rest of our gear and move it out. I want you with me, Krinke. If we run into Krauts, I'd rather talk than fight."

Price said, "I'll go back and get the wireless set."

Conti snapped, "You'll be between Krinke and me, Mister Price. I'd like to be sure of your company all the way. You might say *that's* an order too!"

oo

The WAC secretary picked up the phone on the third ring, and the OSS man she called Howie said, "They pulled it off, Barbara! Zurich just got another report from Snow White. The crazy bastards say they accomplished their mission. No details. But they must have gotten Price in, somehow, and done a job on that damned refinery. Is the general there?"

"I don't know *where* he is! I've called SHAEF a dozen times and he hasn't reached there yet."

"He's probably wandering around in the blackout. You've got to get hold of him, Barbara. The whole thing's fallen apart since those idiots took the bit in their teeth and headed the wrong way! We can't let the Krauts have them! Not now! The bastards *know* too much to fall into the Gestapo's hands!"

"What do you expect *me* to do about it? I'm only a fucking *lieutenant!*"

"Can't you authorize a change in plans, as the general's confidante?"

"Christ, no! He'd have my ass if I ever issued an order in his name behind his back!"

The OSS man said, "I'll send some guys out to find him, Barbara. For Christ's sake, stay by that phone!"

He hung up and turned to another man in a dirty trench coat, saying, "It's no go. She says she's only a fucking lieutenant and that he'd have her ass for it!"

The man in the trench coat smiled thinly and said, "I hear she fucks good, for a lieutenant, and he's had her ass since she started working for the old fart!"

The first OSS man said, " 'Tain't funny, McGee. We're going to have to go over the general's head!"

"*You* go over his head. But count me out, old buddy! I'm not putting my ass in a sling just because some jerk-off paratrooper can't read a map!"

"We could ask the flyboys, as a favor."

"Damn it, we already did, and they say they won't risk a kite without a direct order! Make that a direct order from Hap Arnold. The wing commander just told me to take a flying fuck at a rolling doughnut!"

The OSS man at the desk picked up the phone, started to ask for a number, and slammed it down, saying, "I give up. I just don't know what to do." Then he said, "If we don't get some very high brass to give a lot of orders fast, those poor slobs over there in Germany are as good as dead!"

ooo

It was early for a break. But they were heading down-hill at a fast pace, and in another five minutes, they'd be among the farms of the next valley. A bad place to fall out. Conti clicked his metal cricket and said, "Take ten. No smoking. Pass it on."

Krinke repeated the order to the man behind him, and back along the line, someone moaned, "Oh, my aching back!" and flopped heavily to the forest duff between the trees. Conti moved back along the line, hissing, "Keep it down, goddamn it! We're right up the slope from a fucking village!"

He took a packet from his baggy jump pants and started handing out the benzedrine, warning each man in turn that the pills might make them feel a bit overconfident. He gave one to Gilmore and said, "If you start singing again, I'll bust your ridge-running ass, Gilmore."

Gilmore popped the pill in his mouth, swallowed, and asked, "When can we get rid of this old Kraut, sarge? I swear I'm plum wore out a-draggin' his daid ass!"

Conti said, "I'll have someone spell you. I want to carry both bodies up to the next ridge before we ditch either of them."

"You aim to leave old Murph too, sarge?"

Conti looked at the illuminated dial of his watch before he said, "We may have to. I told Murph we'd take him all the way. But we're making piss-poor time and the two of them are slowing us down."

"Old Murph won't mind, sarge. He was a good old boy and he'd want the rest of us to git away. So why don't I just scoop out a couple of hidey holes and . . ."

"I said the next ridge and I meant it," Conti cut in. "I don't want the Krauts to find them this close to our DZ. I'm hoping if we take them far enough, they won't find them at all!"

"You purely are a neat old cuss, sarge. But I'll allow as how you know what you're a-doin'."

Conti moved on, muttering to himself. "It was nice to know *somebody* thought he knew what he was doing. He was damned if he was all that sure himself! He came to the trooper carrying the R-300 and resisted an impulse to call Zurich again. Every time he used the radio, the Krauts had another chance to get a directional fix on them, and if they hadn't sent a plane to meet them on that distant ridge, there was no point in arguing anymore about it. He'd committed himself now. The rest was up to SHAEF, or maybe God.

He went back to where he'd left Krinke and Price, flopping down beside them. Krinke was on his knees with his jacket over his head, studying the map with a pencil flash. He flicked it off as Conti joined them and said, "We've got to work our way between that next village and a logging camp, sarge. There's a road and railroad line to cross, along with what I sure hope is a shallow stream!"

Conti said, "I know. We hit the road first. Then we ford the stream, go up the railroad bank, and cross 500 yards of open field. The railroad may be patrolled at night. We'll cross there two at a time. One man covers while the other makes his play."

Price said, "For a man who's abso-bloody-lutely crackers, you're certainly getting cautious, mate. You're marching us right to a Nazi prison camp, and you worry about crossing a flaming railway! You *really* must be off your chump!"

"They'll be there to pick us up," said Conti stubbornly.

Price shook his head and said, "Right. There are fairies in the bottom of my garden too! Can't you see the lot of us are *expendable,* mate? We've *done* the perishing job they sent us to do! There's no reason for them to worry about us now. We're only *little* chaps, you see. Nobody gives a damn what happens to the likes of *us!*"

Conti said, "I won't buy that. I won't believe they'd let thirteen guys go down the drain without lifting a finger to help. I told them where we'd meet them and they have a whole night to work something out. The army looks after its own."

"You're crackers, mate. The only people waiting for us will be the flaming Nazis! What will you do *then,* mate? What will you do when you reach that bloody ridge and find there's no bloody plane coming?"

Conti shrugged and said, "If worse comes to worse, I guess it's Little Big Horn time. I made my mind up about that a long time ago. I never joined up to surrender, to *anybody!*"

"You're a rare bird, for an Eyetie, aren't you?"

Conti said, "I used to be Italian, back in South Philly. But I jumped in Italy a couple of times, and you know what? I found out I was American, after all. I've been scared shitless a couple of times. But the only time I was ever surrounded, I shot my way out, GI style."

Price sighed and said, "Well, mate, you'll get your chance to do it again, come morning. Nobody gives a damn about us little chaps. You're going to find that out the hard way!"

Conti said, "I'm betting you're wrong."

Price asked, "What if I'm not?"

Conti thought about that. Then he said, "I guess I'll know I joined the wrong army. That's what I thought this war was all about, you know. I mean, looking out for the little chaps."

○○

The man from the British Home Office stared coldly down at the Russian at the chess board. The Russian moved a pawn and said, "The story you tell me is insane, my friend. I know nothing about this maniac you spoke to at American Embassy. You say he is American service man?"

The English official said, "I put it to you he was one of your agents, Mister Petrovich. I put it to you that you betrayed an Anglo-American mission for reasons that escape me. I am still waiting for an explanation. The Americans have allowed my office to handle the matter for both our governments. I believe they are rather cross with you at the moment. I explained that you and I've had these matters out on other occasions."

The Russian put out a hand to move a knight, changed his mind, and took a pawn with a black bishop. Then he sighed and said, "I would like to help you. But since I know not a single fact about the matter, what can I say?"

The Englishman smiled thinly and suggested, "Why

don't you start with the truth for a change? The Americans are in a towering rage, and Home is quite displeased. I hate to use, ah, *pressure* on a fellow diplomat. But if I have to . . ."

"You *threaten,* old friend? Very well, what do you intend to do, now that you've as much as called me a liar?"

"To begin with," said the man from Home, "we intend to demand your recall, as a spy. A spy, I need not add, who was guilty of a terrible blunder. Perhaps your own government will accept your explanations when you get back to Russia. On the other hand, I understand Comrade Stalin has just asked the Americans for more Lend Lease supplies. I don't imagine he'll be too pleased about the way you've been representing him here in London."

The Russian moved a pawn and said quietly, "That is naked blackmail, my friend."

The Englishman nodded pleasantly and said, "Yes, it is, isn't it?"

The Russian studied the board, not looking up, as he asked softly, "Is this a privileged conversation?"

The Englishman answered, "I don't know. We're in your embassy. How many people do you have listening?"

The Russian chuckled and said, "I shall, how you say, put the cards on table, da?"

"That might well be your best move. Why did you betray Operation Octane to the Germans?"

"It was mistake. OKW was not to learn of mission until it was over. We are sorry as your message was sent too soon. My government also wishes Germans to have no fuel for tanks."

"Keep talking. What was your reason for betraying those Americans at all?"

The Russian moved the knight and said, "Was not to betray Americans. Was, ah, *party* matter. One man on mission was defector from our cause. *He* was only one we were after."

The man from Home nodded and said, "That would be *our* man, Price. I hate to sound sticky about it, Petrovich. But Matt Price *is* a British subject, and an officer of His Majesty to boot!"

"We play games, fellow diplomat. A traitor to any cause must die. You British do not intend to knight Lord Haw Haw when you capture him, do you?"

"Setting Price's checkered past aside for the moment, how do you justify betraying a whole company of American paratroopers?"

"Was not company. Only platoon. Was unfortunate about Americans. But to make omelet, one must break more than one egg. Chance to eliminate Price was too good to pass up for, how you say, innocent bystanders. You will explain this to Americans, eh? That Irisher, Ambassador Kennedy, has no diplomatic skill. He keeps sending bad letters about us to Roosevelt."

The man from Home somehow managed not to vomit as he said, "We'll try to smooth it over this time. But I *do* wish you chaps would stick to one war at a time."

ooo

Conti was gasping for breath, but he stayed on his feet as the men about him flopped to the forest litter on the ridge of the slope they'd just climbed at a grueling pace. He found Krinke and said, "Form a detail and get Murph and the Kraut under at least a yard of dirt. Make sure you don't bury them near one of these game trails. Where's Price?"

Krinke said, "I thought he crossed that last valley with you, sarge!"

Conti clenched his teeth and hissed, "Shit! The fucking Limey bastard's taken off!"

Krinke asked, "Want me to go after him, sarge? He'll have to cross all that open ground before he reaches the trees on the other slope and . . ."

Conti snapped "Negative. We'll never catch him in the dark unless we spread out, and the odds are we'd stumble over a Kraut before we stumbled over that slippery Welshman! We'll just have to hope the Krauts don't catch him on his way to Switzerland."

"We'll be in a fucking mess if they do, won't we, sarge?"

"We're already in a fucking mess. Let's give the guys a three minute break, get rid of the bodies, and start picking up the pace. We're only halfway there and my watch has speeded up on me!"

Conti swallowed a huge gulp of moist mountain air, shook his tired head to clear it, and stayed on his feet to count noses.

Somewhere down the slope he heard a nasal voice, singing. He groaned, "Jesus H. Christ! It's that fucking Gilmore again!"

The voice came nearer, twanging, "There was a damned old hen, and she had a wooden laig, and ever' damned old day, she layed a damned old aig!"

Conti called out, "Knock it off, you crazy asshole!" But the mountaineer continued singing, "She layed a damned old aig, in my daddy's damned old hat, and he took his damned old rifle-gun, and fed her to the cat!"

Gilmore broke off singing to ask, "Who's that a-standin' thar? You'd better answer me in *American,* boy!"

Conti said, "It's me, you stupid motherfucker!" Then he saw Gilmore was not alone and asked, "Who's that with you?"

Gilmore came up to him, along with Matt Price, and said, "I brung Mister Price along, sarge. I reckon he got losted, 'cause he was purely haided the wrong way, down yonder."

Conti heaved a sigh of relief and said, "Gilmore, I love you!"

Matt Price dropped wearily to the ground at Conti's feet, saying, "This bloody sod is balmy! He's got my carbine and I think he gave me a ruddy concussion. My head feels bloody awful!"

Gilmore explained, "He was sort of turnt around and didn't want to come this way. I reckon he must think I'm pretty country, for he kept allowin' as how we'uns should be haided south. He said it was north and all. But I knowed better. I may not have all that much larnin'. But I reckon I know north from south."

Conti stared down at Price and said coldly, "You try that again and I'll kill you."

Gilmore laughed and said, "Shucks, I already *tolt* him that, sarge. I heered what you tolt Krinke about ussen stickin' together and it made pure sense to *me!*"

Conti nodded and said, "I want you to keep an eye on him, Gilmore. If he tries anything like that again, blow his fucking head off!"

Gilmore said, "Make less noise did I use my old knife, sarge."

"Do it any way you have to. Take his boot knife and ammo. Get rid of the extra carbine. But keep the clip as an extra. You'd better bend the barrel around a tree before you bury it."

Price protested, "See here, you can't expect me to muck about in Germany without a single bloody weapon!"

"You stick close to the ridge-runner, here, and you won't need a weapon. You're under arrest, Price. Make another break for it and you're dead!"

Price snorted, "Coo, you can't arrest *me!* What's the charge, premeditated survival?"

"Get some rest and be ready to move in five. We've got a long way to go, Mister Price, and like it or not, you're going with us!"

○○

It was crowded in the pub. The air was blue with tobacco smoke, and a rinky-tink piano was batting out a
boogie-woogie version of "Roll Me Over in the Clover."
The man at the piano was an American GI. But the voices
singing the chorus were mostly British, as they sang, "Oh,
I gave her number nine, and she said, It feels divine! Roll
me over, lay me down, and do it again! Roll me *oh*-ver,
in the *clo*-ver! Roll me over, lay me down, and do it
again!"

The all clear had sounded some time ago. But the Tall
General was working on his seven or eighth pint of Arf n'
Arf, as well as the ATS girl he'd been buying for since
he'd stumbled over her in a booth. The ATS girl was a
bit toothy and more than a little drunk. But she had a
nice little body under that olive drab uniform, and what
the fuck, he was going to catch hell for missing the
briefing anyway.

The ATS girl was pleased with the Tall General's looks
and flattered by his rank. British officers never were this

nice in public to the likes of her. He'd laughed and pinched her under the table when she told him the screwdriver joke. He seemed a dear old thing, and he'd said he'd see about putting in a word at SHAEF about her overdue corporal tapes. . . .

The publican flicked the lights and shouted, *"Time, ladies and gents!"* and the ATS girl said, "Coo! It's almost ten and we have to drink up and leave, just as we was getting acquainted!"

The Tall General said, "It's a hell of a time to close the bars. But listen, I know a private club we can still go to. Over by Trafalgar Square. They serve real booze too. Not this horse piss they call beer over here!"

The girl asked, "Would I be welcome, luv? I mean, I'm only a ruddy lance corporal and you're a flaming officer. It might look odd, was you to take me into a posh west end club."

The Tall General shrugged and said, "We have to go *some* damn place. They're about to toss us out of *this* dump. Where do you suggest?"

"Well, I took a room off Piccadilly, just for this leave. We could go there, I suppose. But mind, you have to promise to be good."

"I'm always good," smiled the Tall General, who knew the rules of the game as played in London. The girl said, "Well, I don't *usually* invite a bloke to my room. But since we're both strangers here in London . . ."

The Tall General said, "I know. You were raised a proper girl. But in a world at war, we have to something or other."

Christ, he was drunk as a skunk. He'd told Barbara he'd call the office before he turned in. But she'd only ask a lot of dumb questions, and what the fuck, Barbara could handle anything that came up.

ΟΟΟΟΟΟΟΟΟΟΟΟΟΟΟΟΟΟΟΟΟΟΟΟΟΟΟΟΟΟΟΟΟΟΟΟΟΟΟΟΟΟΟΟΟΟΟΟΟΟ

The night manager at the hydrogenation plant looked up from his desk as another SS man came in grinning. The SS man held up what looked like a canvas briefcase and said, "Look what we found on one of the cracking towers! Enough TNT to blow us off the map!"

The night manager gasped and said, "God! They *did* get in, after all! I told you there was something funny about those day-shift men vanishing like that, Herr Leutnant!"

The SS man said, "Don't worry. There were only two charges, and we've defused them both. Lucky for us we thought to search for them though. They were set to go off at midnight, and it's almost eleven now!"

A technician came in and said, "Herr Direktor, we're having a little problem with the synthetic oil. There's a lot of inert carbon dust coming through from the catalytic chamber."

The night manager snapped, "Can't you see I'm busy? You must be running too cool. Over there. Raise the temperature 500 degrees and burn it off. The gas is probably sucking soot from the retort."

"Jawohl, Herr Direktor. Have they caught those Amis yet?"

"No. But they will, and the swine failed to hurt us in any case. Just do your job and let us worry about the Americans, eh? We have a lot of fuel to deliver in the next few weeks! I want this plant in full production. So do the best you can about that dust. We can't afford to shut down for a cleaning just now."

○○

It was a little after midnight and they were making better time now. Conti had worried about leading his men along that fire break back there. But the cleared strip through the forest had done two things for him. It had verified his position on the map, and since it ran down hill a good two miles, they'd been able to run all the way.

The benzedrine he'd taken had put new life in his legs. But Conti forced himself to lay down as he gave the men a three minute break. They had more open farmland to cross, and they had to be rested and alert before they risked it. He took the map from Krinke, huddled over it in a clump of woods, and checked it with the pencil flash. He'd been right about the fire break. There was a cluster of houses down the slope. But the farm folks' fields were apparently worked from a single hamlet. There was a mill stream and a secondary road to cross. But at this hour, it would be no sweat. The night had turned cold and misty. The farmers would be in bed by now.

He switched off the little light, tucked the map and

pencil flash away, and said, "We'd better get moving, Krinke."

"You want me to take the point, sarge?"

"No. We'll stick together. It's black as a bitch and I don't want anyone getting separated." He turned and told Price, "We're moving on. Pass it down the line."

They got to their feet and left the tree line, grateful for the mist as they ghosted across a meadow, knee deep in wet grass. They reached the muttering mill stream on their side of the valley road. The water was freezing but shallow, and they gingerly started across. Someone in the column turned his ankle on a wet rock and fell with a mighty splash. There was a rumble of suppressed laughter and Conti hissed, "Quiet! As you were for a minute!"

They froze in place, half of them shin deep in freezing mountain run-off, as Conti counted, "One Mississippi, two Mississippi," to the count of fifty, under his breath. Then he nodded and moved on, satisfied the sound had not attracted attention.

He and Krinke made it to the roadside ditch, as somewhere in the night, a door slammed and a childish voice called out, in a worried tone, "Drachen! Drachen! Wo bist Du, Drachen?"

Conti hissed, "Down!" and dropped beside Krinke in the muddy ditch. The voice came floating up the road. It sounded like a little girl's. Conti nudged the German-speaking Krinke and whispered, "What's she yelling about?"

Krinke said, "She's calling to a pet, I think. I hope to God it's not a fucking *dog!*"

The child came up the road, a misty four-foot outline, as thirteen men cowered in silent desperation along the ditch. The little girl had almost reached them, calling out in childish distress, when a woman in the distance shouted, "Gretchen, komme nach Hause!"

The child peered into the darkness, crying, "Drachen, bist Du es?"

Then her mother repeated her call, in a no-nonsense tone, and the girl turned back, calling, "Ich komme, Mutti!"

Krinke waited until the sound of her footsteps faded before he let out a long sigh and muttered, "I'm sure glad Gretchen listens to her momma!"

Conti said, "Hold it until we hear the door shut. That was close!"

"For us or for the kid?" asked Krinke.

Conti didn't answer as he slid the knife back in his boot sheath. There had to be a way to leave women, kids, and animals out of any war. He heard the sound of a door slamming and said, "Let's go. Walk, don't run, to the nearest exit!"

As he started to rise, there was a sudden blur of motion and something white crashed into his legs, hissing like a snake!

A bone-jarring blow across the knees sent Conti crashing to the earth as Krinke gasped, "I got it! I got it! Jesus Christ, what *is* it!"

Conti rolled, drawing his knife as he saw Krinke's blurred form entangled with a ghostly blur of hissing whiteness. The reptilian hissing ended in a strangled squawk as Krinke stabbed whatever it was a dozen times and jumped to his feet, breathing heavy. Then he stomped the figure at his feet, bent over, and muttered, "I'll be goddamned! I just knifed a fucking *goose!*"

"A fucking *what*?" asked Conti, moving closer.

Krinke laughed wildly and said, "That's who Drachen was! The little girl's pet goose! I never knew a goose could fight like that! I think he busted my fucking nose!"

Conti suppressed an hysterical laugh and said, "Pick it up. We'll ditch it in the next patch of woods. With any luck, she'll think a fox got it, by the time they find it."

Krinke bent over, wiping his upper lip with the free hand as he observed, "Take one tough damned fox to tangle with *this* big bastard!"

Conti said, "Let's go. According to the map, the next five miles should be clear sledding through another patch of woods."

Behind him, Krinke said, "This sure is a mean country. I know now why my grandfolks left. All they ever do in Germany is *fight*. Even the *birds* are fighting sons of bitches!"

○○○

The man who called from the US Embassy sounded angry as he snapped, "What do you mean the general's left for the night? Doesn't he know there's a war on? Kennedy himself is coming at us on a broom! We want to talk to that guy Price! If he doesn't back that crazy story the Russians are putting out, there's going to be changes in Washington's thinking! Zurich says he's with those other poor slobs, somewhere in the middle of the Bavarian Alps. If those damned Nazis get to Price before we do, a lot of very useful information goes with him to the grave. The Krauts won't mess around with Price. They've been after him since Spain! We want that jerk alive. He knows enough about the Commies for *them* to want him dead too!"

The WAC secretary said, "There's nothing I can do without the general, sir. OSS relayed the message those lunatics sent about an air lift. I passed it on to Eighth Air Force *and* the RAF. They say it's just too risky!"

"Did you tell them those men are counting on it?"

"Yes, of course, and they told me to do something I

find anatomically impossible. That was the Eighth, of course. RAF Operations was very polite when they said no."

"Did you try Air Transport Command?"

"Yessir. They asked for an order from the general, in writing."

"Wild Bill Donovan has his own private air force, damn it! Why can't the OSS get a plane in to them?"

"Their nearest clandestine strip is in Italy, flying supplies to the partisans in Yugoslavia. They'd violate Swiss air space, hopping the Alps direct. The Swiss have threatened to shoot down the next Allied plane that flies over a cheese factory, and they have radar coordinated guns to do it too!"

"What's the matter with an end run, over Austrian territory?"

"They have guns too. And night fighters over the Brenner Pass!"

The embassy man said, "I'll see what I can do at this end. Meanwhile, you'd better start looking for that gold-bricking son of a bitch you work for. If the Krauts get to Price before we do, I'm making it my personal business to see that he gets busted to Boy Scout before I'm through with him!"

He slammed down the receiver and pushed a button on another phone, picking it up to snap in a whip-crack tone, "Put me on the transatlantic and get me through to Washington!"

●○●

"This is Snow White calling Bashful. Snow White calling Bashful. Come in, Bashful. Over."

Conti listened as he squatted by the R-300 in a thicket of second-growth poplar saplings. His feet hurt and his legs were killing him. He popped another benzedrine pill in his mouth, hoping it would help and knowing it probably wouldn't. Some of the others were in worse shape than he was, and he was having to break more often now. One of the men had developed a hacking cough in the cold damp dark, and a few yards away, Gilmore was singing again. He kept telling the stupid bastard to shut up. But Gilmore was high as a kite on the benzedrine, and at least he was singing softly about that goddamned Riley's daughter.

He repeated his call and listened to the white noise in the earphone as Gilmore sang, or rather moaned, "Came there a knock upon my doorstep. Who should it be but one-ball Riley. Two horse pistols in his hands, lookin' for the man what shagged his daughter . . ."

A far-away voice crackled, "Bashful to Snow White. Bashful to Snow White. What is your current situation, Snow White? Over."

Conti said, "We've only got a mile or so to go. But it's starting to get light. We'll meet you with three smudge fires. Repeat three smudge fires. Over."

The OSS man in Zurich pleaded, "Negative, Snow White! Repeat, *negative!* We've been trying half the night and it's no go! Repeat, *no go!* Suggest you hole up until it gets dark again. Over."

Conti swore and asked, "Hole up *where,* for Christ's sake? The mothers have cut our trail with dogs. Repeat *dogs!* We've been hearing them in the distance for the past couple of hours. I took a zigzag to make sure, and the mutts changed course with us! I figure we're about five miles ahead of them. But they have our scent and they're on our trail. Let's say they're too dumb to radio on ahead, we can maybe keep ahead of them for now. But when we stop, I'd say we have about an hour before they catch up with us. Over."

There was a long pause. Then the voice in his receiver said, "Suggest you keep moving, then. Make for the original destination. Repeat. You have orders to make for your original destination! Over!"

Pete Conti said an unkind thing about the other's mother and added, "Goddamn it, I told you it was getting *light* out here! We've been running all night and our legs are giving out. We're going to have to make a stand, way in the middle of the air. I don't know how long we can hold them off. But it won't be all that long! What's the *matter* with you fucks? We're not more than an hour away from you, by air! Over!"

The voice from Zurich hesitated before it answered, "I'm sorry, Snow White. There's nothing we can do. You should have followed orders. Over . . . and out!"

Conti shouted, "Don't give me that over and out shit,

damn it! Get me a fucking *plane!* Over!"

There was no reply. Conti switched off the set and hit it with his fist, cracking open a knuckle. Beside him, Krinke said, "Hey, you'll bust the radio, sarge!"

Conti wiped a hand over his face, took a deep breath, and called out, "Gilmore! Shut your fucking face!"

The mountaineer stopped singing, and somewhere off in the forest, a hound bayed hollowly. Krinke's voice was desperately calm as he observed, "I'd say that was four or five miles back, wouldn't you, sarge?"

Conti shrugged and said, "More like three. They're picking up the pace now. It's getting light enough to risk moving faster through the trees."

"For us or them, sarge?"

"Them. We have to slow down to avoid running into another patrol ahead. So let's get moving, shall we? Those fuckers are only thirty or forty minutes behind us!"

ooo

A lab technician at the hydrogenation plant rubbed some synthetic oil on a slide and muttered, "It feels like graphite," as he placed the slide under a microscope. He studied the dark granules in the oil and said, "It's soot. The coal beds must not be properly spread in the retort. Those damned Jews from the camp must have left some lumps in the pulverized coal. You'll have to damp the retort and rake the whole mess out!"

The plant director swore and said, "That will take two days! We have to let the retort cool before even a Jew can work in there, and by the time we lay a proper bed again . . ."

"It can't be helped," insisted the technician. "This shit you've been tapping off is too filthy to feed into the cracking towers. Let's just hope too much of it hasn't been piped through already!"

"Won't it settle out, if we let the fuel sit for a time?"

"In an aircraft's carburetor, it may settle out! It's a very fine suspension. You'll just have to shut down until we find out what's causing it!"

217

○○○

The Horst, common near the Rhine, was an interesting lesson in textbook geography. A huge block of quartzite had been left stranded in the sky as the softer German rocks had eroded away over several million years. Quartzite weathers very slowly to a sterile soil. So the horst was bald of trees as well as flat of top. A meager growth of alpine plants crept up the rocky slopes in an ankle-deep carpet of silvery green. Frost-fractured scree made the slope a harder climb than it looked. But Conti and his men took it at a weary run, cursing and slipping on the treacherous footing. It was almost broad daylight now, and they felt naked on the mountainside as they struggled to the flat top. Krinke was first to reach the summit. He turned, outlined against the morning sky, to shout, "Come on, you guys! Get the lead out!"

A rifle shot echoed from the tree line down the slope, and Krinke spun like a ballerina as the German bullet grabbed him by the shoulder and threw him to the ground. Conti came over the edge, grabbed Krinke's nearest boot, and dragged the wounded trooper with him out of range.

The first shot was followed by the cellophane crackle of small arms fire as the German patrol opened up from the trees below.

Gilmore dropped his carbine and fell forward on his face with a bullet in his back. Matt Price was nearest to the second casualty. He swore and bent to pick the fallen trooper up, holding Gilmore in his arms like a child as he staggered up the scree. Something plucked at Price's pant leg, and another round tore the heel from his right boot as it split the bottom of his foot. He kept climbing in a zigzag stagger and made it to the top as a bullet ticked his left ear. He ran a few steps and flopped with Gilmore to the ground, muttering, "I should have left you for the perishing Jerries!"

Gilmore smiled weakly at him and said, "Thanks, old buddy. That was right neighborly of you."

The others were safely on the summit now, answering the rifle with staccato bursts from their carbines. Conti shouted, "Single fire, damn it! Wait 'til the motherfuckers break cover! We don't have ammo to throw away on *trees!*"

A dark form burst from the tree line and came up the slope at them, barking furiously. Conti shouted, "Hold your fire. I'll get it!" and nailed the Doberman with a single shot. "Teach *you* to sic your dog on me!"

The firing from the tree line faded as a German, apparently, ordered his men to pick their targets carefully. Conti looked up at the empty sky and said, "We'd better start the smudge fires."

Matt Price sat up, rubbing his injured ear, and said, "We'd better start looking for something white to wave too! Those flaming bastards *have* us *now!* What will you bet they're working around to the far side right this very minute?"

Conti nodded and said, "Gordon, De Marco, get over

to the far side and give a holler if you see anything!"
Then he smiled at Price and said, "For a guy who's always
bitching, you did okay just now. How bad was Gilmore
hit?"

"He'll live," grumbled the Welshman. "At least until
those flaming Jerries blow us off the top of this ruddy
hill! You know they'll send for mortars, don't you, mate?"

Conti nodded and said, "We'd better dig in."

Price snorted, "Garn! There's not three inches of soil
on this flaming rock you've trapped us on!"

Conti bent over Krinke and said, "I've got to gather up
some of these weeds and start the fires. How's it coming,
Krinke?"

Krinke said, "It only hurts when I laugh. I'm okay,
sarge. Just get me *out* of here, huh?"

A trooper shouted, "Hey, sarge! There's a guy down
there with a white flag? You want me to shoot him?"

Conti answered, "Let's see if we can keep them busy
talking for a while. Are you up to it, Krinke?"

The wounded man said, "Sure. They didn't shoot me in
the *mouth!*"

Conti and Price helped Krinke to the edge of the Horst
and the German-American shouted down in German,
"Stop where you are, friend!"

The gray-clad German with the truce flag shouted back,
"I can a little English. Surrender! You shall be well
treated."

Conti asked Krinke, "What's that uniform, regular
army?"

Krinke shook his head and said, "That eagle on his
sleeve means Waffen SS. I hear they're *mean* motherfuckers too!"

Conti said, "Stall him. I've got to get those smudge
fires going."

As he crawled away, Price looked up at the sky and

muttered, "Father Christmas is coming too, most bloody likely!"

The German down the slope shouted up, "You are here surrounded and we have sent for Stukas! You know, my friend, what is a Stuka?"

"No!" shouted Krinke. "Tell us about the Stuka, Kraut!"

"A Stuka is a dive bomber. You have no cover from the air, up there. You must surrender *now*, Americans! It will go hard with you if you do not surrender!"

Krinke called down, "How do we know you won't shoot us?"

The German answered, "Because I give you my word, as an officer of the Third Reich! You will come down from that ridiculous place at once, and I promise you will be treated well!"

"We have to radio for permission!" Krinke shouted. "We have orders not to surrender. But if they tell us it's in order . . ."

The German laughed and said, "We know all about your orders, *Snow White!* Yes, you thought we were not listening. But we were. We know you have been abandoned by your friends. Go ahead and call them if you like. But you have not much time. The Stukas will be on you any minute!"

A column of smoke rose from the top of the mountain and the German with the white flag shouted, "What are you burning up there, Americans?"

Krinke shouted, "We're cooking breakfast!"

The German laughed and shouted, "I see you wish to burn your orders before you surrender, eh? Very well, but be quick about it! Once the Stukas start their run up there, it will be too late for you to come down! You shall *die* up there, Americans!"

Conti had three smudges going now, and he crawled back to ask Krinke how it was going. Krinke said, "It's a

Mexican standoff, sarge. He knows they can't come up. But he doesn't think we're going anywhere either. I hope he's bluffing about those fucking Stukas!"

Price said, "He's not bluffing, mates. I think I hear the bloody Stukas *coming!*"

Another man shouted, "I see them! Coming in from west-southwest! Looks like a pair of ME-109s!"

Conti shouted, "Hit the dirt!" and flattened out between Price and Krinke as the fighter planes came roaring in, sunlight from the east horizon glinting on their whirling props. Price's face was pressed against the gritty quartzite soil, and he grunted, "They're Messerschmitts, all right! I met the buggers before, in another war a million years ago!"

The fighters skimmed in over the ridge, lashing the prone men along the crest with the shock waves from their wing tips and stirring up a flying cloud of dust as they passed over and beyond to scream skyward in a climbing turn.

Krinke said, "They never fired a shot!"

"Just you wait!" Price said. "They're pinning us down for the perishing Stukas to make their bomb run! You hear those other engines, coming in from due south?"

Conti rolled on his side, raising the muzzle of his carbine in what he knew was a futile gesture. He felt curiously calm and detached as he remembered another time, in Sicily, when American planes had done this to some enemy troops pinned down in much the same way on another sunny morning. He'd felt sorry for those poor slobs at the time. He wondered absently if the Germans down the slope were feeling sorry for him!

The throbbing engines came down at them, as Conti searched the sky for the inverted gull wings of a Nazi Stuka. Then he saw the plane, a big low-winged job with twin engines. It was coming right at him, wing tips wavering as it lost speed. It was coming in too low and slow for a bombing run. It was . . . *landing,* for Christ's sake!

Conti jumped to his feet, waving, as he shouted, "Hold your fire! It's a fucking C-47! It's one of *ours!*"

The fighter planes had reached the top of their climbing turn and rolled over, square wing tips black against the sky. Someone shouted, "Here come the ME-109s again!" and Conti chortled, "One-o-nines your ass! Those are P-51s! It's a fighter escort! Everybody up and let's get the fuck *out* of here!"

The lumbering C-47 touched down and hit its brakes, rolling to a stop a hundred yards away. Price got Krinke to his feet as another two men picked Gilmore up and carried him toward the transport. The two Mustangs flashed over, wigwagging their wing tips as they continued on to snarl into the trees downslope with their guns. A door near the wing root of the C-47 popped open, and a crew member appeared in the square of darkness, shouting, "Drop your cocks and grab your socks! We can't hang around all day for you assholes!"

The wounded men were pushed and hauled aboard as Conti stood by on the ground. He was laughing like a madman, punching men on the shoulders as they scrambled aboard. Price was next to last, and Conti kicked him joyously in the seat of the pants as the Welshman scrambled up through the opening. Then Conti pulled himself up, flopping face down on the perforated metal deck as the crew member pulled his legs in and slammed the cargo door shut with a curse. The engines roared and the big plane leaned forward against its brakes, held in place until the props revved up to full power. The pilot released the brakes, and the C-47 lurched forward, gaining almost enough speed to take off, but dropping ominously as they reached the far end of the mountain.

And then the big kite's wings caught hold of the sky, the tail fell almost into a stalling attitude, and they were airborne!

The transport circled as the men who could manage struggled to the windows. Conti looked out and felt his stomach lurch as he found himself staring straight out at a vertical wall of moving treetops. Then the treetops fell away from view and they were flying even keel, due south.

He caught at a crew member crawling past and shouted, above the roaring engines, "Where are we going?"

The crew member shouted back, "Bari! They sent us up from Italy after you jerk-offs! Let go my fucking arm! I gotta get back to my regular job!"

Conti hung on, shouting, "Two of my people need a medic! You got a first aid kit aboard?"

"I'll bring you one, later. I gotta get to the radio right now!"

Conti let go and relaxed in the bucket seat by the window. It was going to be all right. He'd done it. He was taking his people home.

He shouted, "Buckle up!" and fastened his seat belt. Price joined him, shouting above the engines, "You were right, Mate! I thought you were crackers. But you were right as rain! I guess somebody cares about us little chaps, after all!"

Pete Conti didn't answer. He was on his way to a medal, and a generation of his men's children were about to be raised on the legend of Iron Wop Conti, the toughest son of a bitch in the Eighty-Second Airborne. But this was all in the future. Conti was going to be twenty years old in six weeks.

So Iron Wop Conti, the toughest son of a bitch in the Eighty-Second Airborne, buried his face in his hands and began to cry.